CRYPTIC MAGIC

THE HIDDEN PROPHECY TRILOGY BOOK 1

LILY SKYY

Cryptic Magic
Copyright © 2021 by Lily Skyy
www.LilySkyy.com

Second Edition: March 2022

ISBN 978-1-956525-03-8 (ebook)
ISBN 978-1-956525-88-5 (paperback)

Published by Books to Hook Publishing, LLC.
www.BooksToHook.com

CONTENTS

PROLOGUE

RHAPTA

Tahir stood at the end of the Grand Hall, looking out onto the city of Rhapta. The wide, sweeping steps fanned out below him, but he did not descend. No, he would not do that. He belonged in the Grand Hall as all Elders did in times of strife. He stood positioned in the middle of the last two pillars and looked out.

The limestone city spread out before him in near-perfect symmetry, with the Grand Hall at the head of the central plaza. The only structure more grand was the magalkan'a that sat in the center of the Plaza itself. The massive, azure stone nearly pulsed with energy, and people flocked daily to place their hands upon its warm surface.

It has been confirmed, said a voice like darkness in his mind. A moment later, a shadow of a man materialized at Tahir's shoulder; the light coming in from the archway seemed to shy away.

Tahir let out a long, deep sigh. He had spent years of his

life, close to a century, devoting time and effort to protecting his people. All the Elders did, but him more so than others; whether or not they knew that. He prided himself in being able to make the difficult decisions the other Elders refused to do, and he would do so again.

You are sure? he asked. He had to be sure. The resources he had devoted to uncovering secrets long buried would boggle the mind of a lesser man, but he knew what knowledge costs.

Yes, he is, the voice replied back. The man waited patiently for his orders. He would wait until the sun set and rose again a hundred times or until starvation eventually took him. Obedience had been the heart of their training. But Tahir needed him a while longer and found no use in letting him rot.

Take care of it then.

The shadow man moved to leave.

Oh, and Yusuf? Tahir said, turning to look over his shoulder. The shadow man paused. *Be sure to get there before the boy.*

The shadow man gave an almost imperceptible nod and vanished into the pools of darkness that led deeper into the Grand Hall.

Tahir took another breath and let the familiar iciness loose. It crept down his legs to crackle over the marble floor. Frost spread around him in fractal patterns, traveling up the pillars to the sides of the room. The release felt good, and he reveled in the feeling.

It would be his last bit of peace for quite a while.

CHAPTER I
TWISTING SHADOWS

"Ladies, are you finished with the toilets yet?" Karin asked for the third time in ten minutes. Kinza didn't have to look; she knew her boss was standing just outside the public bathroom, nose wrinkled because cleaning stalls were above her. The delight of scrubbing corporate toilets was bestowed upon newer employees, if Kinza's three and a half years as a cleaner could be considered "new."

"Yes, your grace. We'll be out in just a moment," Mitra said in a singsong voice from the next stall over. Kinza sniggered at the tone. Mitra had been hired a few months after Kinza, both of them fifteen at the time, and they had quickly become friends, commiserating over their shared disdain of Karin's micromanaging tendencies.

Mitra had a tendency to lighten the gloomy atmosphere that Karin created. The few months prior to her starting, Kinza had worked with another older girl who liked to put headphones in and listen to music on full blast their entire shift. It's not that Kinza minded, but it was a bit lonely with no one to talk to. Mitra had a way of making the time fly by whenever she was around.

The job didn't have the greatest pay either, but finding a good job at their age was difficult with so many other teenagers in the area, and both girls had needed the money. So for the past few years, cleaning corporate offices in downtown Chicago after school had been bittersweet.

Tonight's client was a small health food organization that rented office space in one of the fancy high rises. Wood paneling, infinity sinks, eco-friendly coffee machines, it smelled of high-end luxury. They had different clients most days of the week. Every Tuesday, Karin and her team would show up after the employees had left, and the three of them wouldn't get out until close to nine.

Karin just snorted and put an imaginary hair back into her bun. She always came to work with her light brown hair in a bun so tight it made her already harsh features almost menacing. After assigning the two girls the more difficult tasks, she always left the ones that required the least physical effort for herself. So when their shifts ended, her clothes were never wrinkled, and she never had a drop of sweat on herself. "I'm vacuuming the section by the elevator, and then I'm leaving, so you had better be done by then," she said, and Kinza heard her retreating footsteps down the hall.

She didn't have the energy to throw a retort back; she was exhausted from another nightmare, the sixth in the last week. Who knew that you could be tired when you were both awake and asleep? The nightmare was always the same. She was crawling past a barrier of shimmering air, dense forest around her, and a flat-topped mountain in the distance. She never knew why she had to go; she just did. As soon as she got past the barrier, the scene shifted. There were twisting, dark shapes in a vast room of god-like statues and marble floors. She remembered they were marble because the moonlight would glint off the floors from the skylight above. Something sinister emanated from the cluster of dark shapes, an intention that left her skin feeling oily and her chest heavy the morning after. Unable to speak or move, she would just watch them until suddenly they would all turn to her, eyes boring directly into her. That's when she would wake up and still feel as if they were watching her.

"I swear, she thinks we've never done this before," Mitra said, popping her head into the stall Kinza was cleaning. She had waist-length, raven hair in a braid and long, dark eyelashes framing deep brown eyes. It was ridiculously unfair how good she looked, even after hours of work cleaning toilets, emptying the garbage, and hauling vacuums up and down stairs.

Kinza just rolled her eyes. "Clearly," was all she said. She flushed the soap down the toilet and grabbed her bucket, but Mitra was blocking her way out of the stall, hands on her hips. An all-knowing look was on her face. Honestly, Mitra could read her like a book, so it wasn't too far off. When Kinza wanted to vent, it was great, but when she just wanted to close up like a clam, Mitra was there, trying to pry the pearl out for her own good.

"You had one of those nightmares again, didn't you? You don't even need to say it; you have the *worst* bags under your eyes. I could sell those as knock-off Gucci and retire early. You know my mom has this really good tea you can—"

"Sheeeesh, Mitra. Relax, I'm all good," Kinza said, shouldering past her out of the stall. Of course, she had only vaguely mentioned it a few days ago, and now Mitra was trying to single-handedly cure her of all possible ailments. It was touching, but sometimes she could be smothering. She walked by the enormous backlit mirrors on the way out of the bathroom.

Glancing at her reflection, she realized Mitra was right, though; dark circles ringed even darker eyes. It didn't help that the fluorescent lighting washed out her normally soft brown skin. Before she had left for school that morning, she had scraped her hair into a low, sleek ponytail at the nape of her neck. Unlike Mitra, Kinza had to spend hours flat ironing her usual curls to get them to be that straight. But now, at the end of the day, errant strands stuck to her face, and the ponytail was coming halfway out.

"Well, you look like poop. So I beg to differ," Mitra said, hauling their stuff out of the bathroom to meet Karin by the elevators.

Kinza laughed. "Poop? Who says poop? Whatever, let's just get out of here. I have so much homework to do tonight." She followed Mitra through the halls to the lobby by the elevators where Karin was waiting, wrapping up the vacuum cord. On the way, they passed by a wall of floor-to-ceiling windows, and up on the tenth floor, they had a spectacular view of down-town Chicago at night. This high up, you couldn't see any of the grittiness, just the neon lights of the city's nightlife, the reflection off Lake Michigan, and the ever-present flow of traffic on the expressway.

"Didn't you just start classes a week ago?" Mitra asked.

"Yeah, but apparently, there's no 'easy first week' with college courses," Kinza said, throwing up air quotes. "We've already had two quizzes. I'm going to die," she said dramatically.

"Yikes," Mitra grimaced.

Both girls had graduated last June, and while Mitra was taking a gap year to save up money, Kinza had started on her bachelor's degree at National Louis. The four-year scholarship into the Human Services program wasn't entirely a surprise with Kinza's 4.0 GPA and an extensive list of volunteer and extracurricular hours, but it had her dancing around the kitchen when the acceptance email had come through. Grams had tried to hide her happy tears but failed miserably. Before they died, Kinza's parents had wanted her to go to college, but with almost no money left behind, the prospect had been bleak. Life had decided to put her into "Difficult Mode," but she wasn't about to let that stop her.

The three of them switched the lights off and took the elevator down to the main lobby. They waved at Phil, the night security guard on the way out. Phil was in his late forties, a single dad from a nasty divorce. He had the belly of someone who spent their evenings drinking beer and eating frozen dinners in front of the tv. He loved his kids, though, and frequently worked doubles so he could buy them nice things. The last thing he wanted was for his kids to get teased for being poor as he had been when he was young.

Kinza knew all of this because he would talk her ear off as she and Mitra waited for Karin to arrive on Tuesdays. He was always nice to them and held the door if he saw them coming and waved goodbye when they were done.

The girls lugged their stuff to Karin's van parked down the street just a few minutes before the meter was set to expire.

"All right, ladies, great work tonight, but let's try to finish a little earlier tomorrow, yeah?" Karin said. As if they hadn't been trying to finish as early as possible already.

"Uh, yeah, sure thing, Karin," Kinza said. She had to scrape the bottom of the barrel to muster even that bit of enthusiasm. She and Mitra grabbed their bags and sweatshirts from the van and waved goodbye, heading down the street to the bus stop. Kinza pulled the ponytail out of her hair, letting the strands flow freely.

"Sure thing, Karin," Mitra mocked, shaking her braid back and forth.

"Finish a little earlier tomorrow, *yeah*?" Kinza mocked back, shaking her head like Mitra, making her hair flip.

Both girls looked at each other and erupted into hysterical laughter. As soon as one would calm down, the other would start up again, and it would take them until the end of the block before they could utter another word without giggling. A few people looked at them in annoyance as they walked by, but they didn't care. It was Chicago, and everyone was annoyed.

They stopped at the bus stop, Mitra pulling out her phone to show her the Instagram pictures of the guy she was currently talking to. She had been telling Kinza about him earlier before Karin had told them to "chat less and work more." "Seriously, Kinz, look at him. He's so *preeettty*." She sighed. Mitra was constantly on a hunt for a boyfriend; she had five just in high school. Kinza didn't know how anyone could even like that many people.

Kinza looked at the shirtless picture of a guy about their age, brown hair perfectly coiffed, sitting in the leather seats of a car that he clearly couldn't afford. He had a jawline that could cut glass. "Okay, yeah. He's cute. What does he do?"

"Umm…" Mitra swiped to another picture, orange nails flashing across the screen.

"He has a job, right? Or is he in school or something? Anything?" Unfortunately, Mitra attracted a very specific type of guy. The kind that had all the charm of a goldfish and rode on good looks and the silver spoon they were born with. Kinza didn't know what she saw in them.

Mitra just gave her a look that said *I don't really care about that.*

"Nope! Hard pass," Kinza said. "He's clearly a player, Mitra." The bus pulled up, and they got on. It was pretty empty. Two older men sat on the left, and a woman and a baby were on the right. The girls sat about halfway to the back, avoiding the seat with the stain, and the bus lurched forward, taking them out of downtown and toward the west side of the city.

"I don't see you tryin' to find somebody. Don't you want a boyfriend? You and Max broke up over a year ago." Images of gorgeous green eyes and a dazzling smile flitted across Kinza's vision. Max had been her high school sweetheart. When they had started dating freshman year, he had doted on her, bringing her flowers and chocolates to school all the time. When he had gotten a license (and a shiny car from Daddy), he had picked her up every day and drove her to school. He always told her how pretty, and beautiful, and cute, and *sweet* she was. She was fairly certain that was the only thing he liked about her because all she could remember now was Max's irritated tone anytime she raised her voice or laughed too loud. They had ended the relationship last year, Max stating that he needed to think about his future and he would need someone a bit more "reserved." Kinza was pretty sure he wanted a throw pillow for a girlfriend. Silent and decorative.

The breakup had stung, though. She missed having someone who would laugh at her jokes and eat the pickles she didn't like, and someone who believed in her. After her parents had died ten years ago, she decided she wanted to change the world. She wanted to house the homeless, feed the poor, establish better education for inner-city kids, the works. Max had told her it was a pipe dream, and human services careers didn't make nearly enough money. Either way, when she and Max had started dating, she had thought she had the perfect relationship. It was a pretty picture for a little while, but she refused to be a trophy, even if Max's distasteful expression came up anytime she made herself heard.

"When do I have time for a boyfriend? I have four classes worth of homework to do, then I have to get back up tomorrow for school, and then we are working tomorrow night again. I look like I haven't showered in months, and I'm pretty sure this is a bleach stain on my sleeve," she said, picking at the threads of her gray sweatshirt.

"Girl, we both know damn well that given a nap, a shower, some makeup, and a change of clothes and you would be the hottest person, like, ever!" Mitra said, throwing a hand up. Kinza knew she was exaggerating but appreciated the effort she put in. She just rolled her eyes and rested her head on Mitra's shoulder.

As they moved further west out of downtown, the shiny high rises gave way to the trendy neighborhoods of the Chicago Loop. Shops, restaurants, parks, and some smaller apartment buildings passed by the bus windows. That would eventually fade to the areas of Section 8 housing and broken down parks. People were still outside this late, enjoying the last bit of nice weather in early September. As Kinza was looking out the window, she felt the back of her neck tingle. It was probably just the wind blowing through the open window, but on instinct, she whipped her head around, slapping a hand to her neck.

There was nothing there.

But to her surprise, someone sat at the back of the bus. *That's odd,* she thought to herself. *I know I didn't see anyone else behind us when we got on. Maybe he had been lying down.* It wasn't unusual for the occasional drunk person to be seen passed out on the back seats late at night. But this person didn't look drunk. He was wrapped in swaths of dark material from ankle to wrist. It looked like both pants and shirt could have been made from a single bolt of fabric. A hood hung low over his eyes, and a mask pulled up over his nose. Kinza could *feel* him looking at her, though. The light seemed to bend away from him as if repulsed, casting the back of the bus into shadow. She honestly couldn't tell what he looked like with how covered he was. Maybe it was some new tech-wear style. She tried to keep up with current fashion trends, but her budget kept her on a strict leash.

She quickly turned back around.

"What?" Mitra asked, looking at her and then throwing a quick glance over her shoulder. Mitra didn't seem to think anything of the man.

"Nothing, just a mosquito or something," Kinza replied. But for the next few stops, she could feel eyes burning into her back, goosebumps running up her spine. It took all her effort not to turn around. Something about him just felt *off*.

Growing up in Chicago's west side had taught her how to handle herself and recognize when she was in a shady situation. While her neighborhood was relatively safe, any big city had its downfalls, creepy stalkers being one of them.

In third grade, a friend of hers had gotten beat up on the way home from school one evening. The group of older kids had come out of nowhere. She had learned to always walk home with another person whenever she could. When she turned fifteen, she started getting catcalls from sleazy men as she walked to the bus stop. After that, she kept a little switchblade with a plastic green handle in her purse just in case. She had never needed to *use* it, but it made her feel better to have it on her.

Mitra got off a few stops later, promising to find her a boyfriend by the end of the month. Kinza, still distracted, absentmindedly said, "Yeah, sure."

The little squeal Mitra let out pulled her back to the present, and she realized too late that she was going to be receiving a slew of profiles later that evening.

As the bus pulled away again, Kinza looked into the window's reflection, hoping to catch a glimpse of the shadowy person, but couldn't see anything. She slinked a little lower and casually peeked over her shoulder, feigning adjusting her hair.

There was no one there. *Maybe they had gotten off?* She sent a quick text to Mitra, telling her to let her know when she got home safe. Mitra texted back almost immediately that she would.

She relaxed a little now that the person was gone. Moving her hand under her shirt, she scratched lightly at the tattoo on her upper abdomen. It was a palm-sized mandala with two smaller circles in the center that looked like symbolic eyes. The whole thing was surrounded by delicate chains and inked gems that stretched to the sides of her stomach. Her parents had told her they had taken her to get it when she was little, but it had been there for as long as she could remember. And there was no way any licensed tattoo artist in the state of Illinois would tattoo a child. She had given up asking her parents for the truth and just accepted it as a sort of birthmark instead. Sometimes it would tingle softly, just like the back of her neck had only a few minutes before.

She got off two stops later and threw her light blue backpack over her shoulders. The bus stop was at the corner of a small park. The next block up was a short strip mall with a smoke shop, a liquor store, and a nail salon. Her house was a block around the corner from there. She knew the entire neighborhood like the back of her hand and started on her walk home.

It only took her a few steps before the tingling sensation returned to the back of her neck. She kept her head up and looked around her. There was no one behind her. The only light was from a street lamp across the park.

For a second, she thought she saw a shadow move underneath the light. It was probably a stray cat or something. She'd seen a few wandering around recently.

She walked a little faster and crossed the street to the strip mall. She went across the parking lot of broken asphalt to the awning hanging over the storefronts, wanting to stay in the light. The stores were just closing up, the employees locking their doors and heading to their cars. The tingling feeling never left her neck. Just to be safe, she reached back and palmed the little switchblade from her backpack and pulled her sleeves down over her hands. It was a little big on her anyway.

As she passed the nail salon, she heard a scraping movement from the top of the building's awning. Her head snapped up, but of course, she only saw the underside of the awning. Heart beating faster, she looked around again.

There.

Through the shop window's reflection, she could see someone walking on the sidewalk on the other side of the parking lot, in pace with her own reflection. She glanced over out of the corner of her eye.

It was him, the guy wrapped in dark fabric, the light from the streetlamps fizzling out as he walked by. He was openly looking at her now, even though she couldn't see his eyes under the hood.

Kinza's heart started pounding in her chest. She knew when she was being followed but knew better than to run. She had seen too many Animal Planet documentaries where the moment the gazelle took off, the lion bounded across the grass only to reach the frightened animal in a few leaps, snapping its neck in its powerful jaws.

To hell with being a gazelle. She planned on being a tiger in a gazelle suit. Albeit, a *frightened* tiger in a gazelle suit.

Once she rounded the corner of the liquor store, she would only have another block until her house, and Grams always kept the outside light on until she got home. She picked up her speed, looking around to see if anyone else was around. There was a group of people in someone's backyard a few houses away, but it sounded like a party. Music boomed out of old, crackly speakers. They most likely wouldn't be able to hear her if she screamed. The parking lot was almost entirely empty now.

The corner of the store was just up ahead. She looked to her left, keeping her eye on the figure, and she turned right, around the corner.

She slammed into a human wall of muscle and stumbled back a step. Gasping, she looked up, and for a moment, she thought the dark figure had materialized in front of her. But when the person grunted and twisted away from her, she realized it was just a man in a zip-up, black hoodie pulled low. He was way too tall to be the figure she had seen on the bus, who had only looked to be a few inches taller than her. When he didn't immediately grab her, she mumbled a quick, "Watch it," and kept moving.

As she got further away from the strip mall and onto her block, she worked on moving her stomach out of her throat and back to where it belonged. She admonished herself for not even thinking of the knife as she ran into the man. Peering over her shoulder, she looked to see if the dark figure was still following her, but no one was there, just the empty street.

She sighed in relief but kept her ears open the rest of the way home.

NOTHING about this job was going as planned. And Zaid *hated* when things didn't go as planned.

Climbing back up to the roof of the liquor store, he watched the girl walk down the street, steps hurried. He should have taken her when she ran into him, but something about the past week had been off. In the seven years he had been *venari,* a bounty hunter, he had never screwed up a target, and he wasn't about to.

He had been tailing her for the past week, following her around the city and back to her house. It typically took a week, max, to take down a group of ubir. Maybe two days for a single, but never this long for just one. The first thing that threw him was the lack of Aura. Every ubir he had ever encountered had an Aura that radiated shattered, chaotic energy. Their thoughts were always unguarded and erratic, standing out from silent human minds like rabid dogs in a field of sheep. The longer they had been ubir, the more shattered and corrupt their minds became.

But her Aura was silent. It was like she wasn't Anunnaki at all. Just human.

The second thing was *another* Aura coming from across the parking lot. Her daily routine had been down to the minute, but as she walked home tonight, something had changed. As far as Zaid knew, there weren't any other *venari* in the area; they always worked alone, there were no longer enough of them to work in pairs. But there was clearly a steady Aura coming from the other figure. When Zaid had reached out with his own Aura, keeping it visually restrained, he was met by a mind wrapped in an iron-clad fortress. They weren't letting him in. Anunnaki customs dictated they should at least acknowledge each other, regardless of his distaste for unnecessary communication.

The last thing that made this target so odd was he was given a name.

Kinza Solace.

He had never been given a specific name before. His direct superior would always provide a city, an age, and a list of potential abilities to watch out for if they were known. That's it. This time the name and city were the only things he was given. If he had to guess, it must have been because this ubir was particularly dangerous. He had a hard time picturing the girl being more dangerous than a chihuahua. He knew that some of them had abilities to hide in plain sight, veil their Auras, and even compel the minds of the humans around them. Ubir kept their abilities from when they were still Anunnaki; they were just more unstable, deadly even. Hence the need for *venari*.

Zaid ground his teeth in frustration, making his jaw ache. The pain had him focusing again. He cocked his head as if to listen but instead settled into a familiar routine, feeling for the heartbeats in the area. He had done this a thousand times in his life and would easily do it thousands more. The ability was one of the many reasons he was so good at his job. He didn't have much in life, but at least he was damn good at what he did.

He waited until he could feel the steady pulses from the houses around the neighborhood, tens of them coming from inside homes, in cars that passed by, and a group of them clustered outside in a nearby backyard, some obnoxious music blaring out of broken speakers. He felt the heartbeat of the girl walking down the street, away from him. The other dark figure's heartbeat vanished with its owner, melding into the shadows as soon as they had noticed Zaid's own Aura.

He had no intention of following them. He was ready to be done with this stupid target.

Moving across the rooftop to jump down the back of the building, he moved faster than the human eye could track, jumping over fences, into backyards, sticking to the shadows.

Catching up to the girl took moments. He watched her from her own backyard as she turned to open the gate, walk up the path up the stairs, and enter her house.

Crouching, he waited, silent as the midnight wind with his back to the right of the kitchen window. It was cracked less than an inch. He knew because he had done it himself earlier that day, waiting until the old lady took her afternoon nap to pull it open. Settling to the ground, Zaid waited, ear cocked to the window, to listen for his target's name. He wanted to verify it was her one last time before he took her back to Rhapta.

CHAPTER 2

NIGHTMARES OF LIGHT

K inza pushed the gate of the chain-link fence open, letting it clatter shut behind her. Even though she didn't see anyone else the rest of the way home, she still wanted to get inside. You never knew who was out and about, lurking in the bushes.

The house was small, one-story with an attic—a few worn concrete steps leading up to a small porch. A bay window looked out onto the front lawn. Grams had taken the meager grass space and turned it into a wild garden, unchecked hydrangeas, ferns, sunflowers, and something that looked suspiciously like a weed crept over onto the edge of the sidewalk. A little gnome was barely visible between the tall stems by the fence.

She jogged up the steps and let herself in, touching the swirling carving in the doorframe as she went inside. It looked like a series of overlapping infinity signs, with no clear beginning or end. She had no idea if it was actually lucky, but it had been there for as long as she could remember. Once, when she was twelve, she touched the carving before school, praying that she would do well on her math test. A week later, she got the results back; a perfect one hundred. Now she touched it every time, just in case. The screen door creaked as it closed, and she immediately threw the deadbolt into the lock and breathed a sigh of relief.

"Baby, is that you?" Grams called from the kitchen.

"Yeah, I'm gonna change real quick!" she called back, stepping into the hall. It was only the two of them, but the small spaces made them get creative with what they had. The front entry had shoes piled under a short bench covered in boxes, mail, plastic bags, and some of Kinza's school books. Cases of pop sat on the floor next to it, and an overflowing coat rack hung up above, with an umbrella lying crosswise on the hooks. Kinza kicked her worn sneakers under the bench and shuffled to her room to change. She hated wearing her dirty clothes from the day in the house.

The front hall opened to the living room on the right, with the bay window looking out front. Dated but dangerously comfortable sofas faced a flat-screen tv on the side wall. Bookshelves with a hodgepodge collection of items stuck in at strategic angles stood to one side. In them were her parents' books, picture frames of them and Kinza when she was little, a medal from a spelling bee she had won in eighth grade, a picture she had drawn when she was ten, and a forgotten grocery list.

She kept going straight down the hall, passing the bathroom first and then into her bedroom on the left. Grams' bedroom was just after, and at the end of the hallway was the backdoor.

After a quick change into a pair of men's boxers that she bought just for comfort and an oversized t-shirt, she walked down the hall to the right and into the kitchen. Like the rest of the house, it was compact, but it was Kinza's favorite room.

Knick-knacks hung on the bright yellow walls that her mother had painted fifteen years prior. She had faint memories of sitting on the floor while her parents had slapped a few tester colors on the wall. There was a little window over the sink, looking out on the backyard, and a wooden table pushed up against the adjacent wall.

Grams was sitting at the table, hair wrapped up in a silk scarf, tying dead flowers with bits of twine. She liked to take the dead flowers and hang them on the ceiling, saying that it made her feel like she lived in a little fairy cottage. Kinza never made fun of her, even when the dried petals drifted down to collect on the linoleum.

"Lasagna in the fridge," she said, not looking up.

"Mmm." Kinza hummed, opening the fridge and pulling out a huge slab of lasagna before sticking the whole thing in the microwave. She sat down across from Grams and dropped her head into her arms.

"That bad, huh?" Grams asked.

Kinza just groaned into the table before flipping her head up. When she was little, she swore that Grams was an other-worldly, all-knowing being. She always seemed to know how Kinza was feeling, even if she hadn't uttered a single word. Grams used to have Band-Aids ready when Kinza came back inside from being out all day, knowing that she would have scrapped her ankle on her bike pedal. On days when Kinza had given herself a stomach ache from worrying over her grades, Grams had a cup of ginger-chamomile tea hot and ready when she came home. She was always *there*, especially during the hardest times in Kinza's life.

She remembered having a relatively happy childhood and parents that were strict but loving. They never had much for money, but it was enough to get by. Grams had always lived with them, babysitting when both her parents were at work.

There was always someone around for Kinza to talk to, to laugh with, or on rare occasions, to argue with. The four of them would crowd in the kitchen on weeknights, everyone trying to get a bite to eat before bed, Kinza giggling at the chaos. But that was before.

She knew from the fact that the memory came up over and over and from the fact that she couldn't ever tamp it down, it was a symptom of post-traumatic stress disorder. She'd looked it up once, and there it was, nicely labeled with a neat row of symptoms. Knowing the word for it didn't make her feel any better, though. She had gone through therapy, seen counselors, but it couldn't erase the past.

On birthdays and holidays, she would sometimes fall asleep with the memory of Grams sobbing in the hallway, yelling at Kinza to go back outside. She had been nine, playing down the street at the park with her friends. Stomach rumbling for lunch, she ran home, hoping to get her dad to make her a PB&J with slices of banana. All she found was Grams crying on the floor, frantically waving at her to get out. She remembered being so confused, never having seen Grams like that before.

On her way back out the door, she caught a glimpse of her mother's hand poking out from the living room; her ever-clean fingernails curled into her palm. The police sirens could be heard around the neighborhood just a few minutes later.

That night, after what seemed like a hundred people had been in and out of the house, after police officers had asked her a million questions, after the bodies had been wheeled into a van, Grams had taken her to a family friend's house for the night. They slept there in the same bed, and Grams had told her that her parents had been murdered.

Kinza had known what that meant, but it didn't stop her from being confused. Why would anyone murder her mother?

The same woman that sang at the top of her lungs every time her favorite American Idol star came on? Why would anyone murder her father? The same man who would nod stoically along with her mother when she scolded her but would sneak her a candy bar under her door afterward? She couldn't wrap her mind around it, and the detectives never found the suspect either. The absurdity of it had made her angry.

It took until her tenth birthday for the grief to fully hit her when she realized that her parents were never going to sing "Happy Birthday" to her ever again. She bawled in Grams' lap for hours that day, letting out months of pent-up sorrow. Over the years, the anger and sadness eventually turned into grit, and grit eventually grew into determination. The word the counselors used was "resilient," and she knew that was true. While she was resigned to the fact she would never know *why* her parents were killed, she fully intended on living a life that would make her parents proud.

Well, she tried anyway.

Right at that moment, with four classes worth of home-work, Karin's "gentle" request to work harder tomorrow, and the smell of reheated lasagna, she was struggling a bit.

Kinza launched out of her chair, hoping that the food hadn't splattered too much in the microwave. Grams would have her scrubbing the whole thing for hours if she did. "I just have a lot of homework," she said.

"I was talking about those nightmares," Grams replied, gathering bundles of dead flowers together.

Kinza froze, fork halfway to her mouth as she stood in the middle of the kitchen. "Ugh, you noticed? I didn't think I was making that much noise."

"Baby, I'll wake up from a pin drop clear across town. I sure as hell can hear you tossing and turning and blabbering in your sleep." Grams looked over, eyeing her from head to toe with a knowing expression. "It'll be over soon. Just drink more of that lavender tea I left on the counter there." Kinza looked over, and sure enough, a steaming mug of faintly purple tea sat by the toaster. She supposed she came home at the same time every Tuesday, but the fact that it was the perfect temperature at that exact time was impressive.

"How do you know it'll be over soon? I'm pretty sure they are getting worse, not better. Maybe I'm allergic to that tea or something." She sat down across from Grams again, and a few strands of hair reached down into her lasagna, so she shoved them back.

"No, no. Just drink the tea. It'll be fine," Grams said cryptically, brushing loose petals into a pile.

"Do all nigtmurrs get bebber beffo they gep worf?" Kinza said with a mouthful of lasagna.

"Chew your dang food, girl." Grams laughed. She stood up to place her dried flowers in the corner where a few other bundles waited to be hung up.

Kinza finished her food and washed her plate in the sink, letting it dry on the rack. She had decided to just get up early to do her homework. "All right, I'm, like, stupid tired, so I'm going to head to bed. Night, Grams," she said, kissing her on the cheek. She headed to her room.

"Kinza?" Grams said.

Kinza popped her head back around the corner. "Ya?"

"Drink your tea." Kinza dutifully grabbed the mug and gulped it down. After a quick trip to the bathroom, she shuffled back to her room. Her bedroom was the smaller of the two, Grams had the master, but she liked the coziness of hers. Tangerine walls that she had painted herself made the room look bright all the time. Her bed was shoved into the corner, with a mound of pillows and blankets on top. On the other side of the room was a desk littered with homework, makeup, a flat iron, and an old dresser sat next to it. Pieces of jewelry scattered the top around papers, loose change, way too many hair products, and a picture of her and her parents on Christmas when she was little. Grams said her room looked like a bomb went off, but Kinza considered it to be more like ordered chaos. Things were exactly where she needed them to be.

Just before climbing into bed, the faint tingling sensation returned. Out of caution, she walked over to the window above her nightstand and parted the blinds, peering out.

She saw nothing but the chain-link fence surrounding their yard, the house next to them, and a sliver of the street, illuminated by the nearby streetlamp. Even at this time of night, she could hear a dog barking, neighbors yelling from two houses down, and the faint sound of an ambulance on the expressway.

As she pulled away, though, a shadow flitted across the street.

She pulled the blinds wider, trying to see. After a few more moments, eyes roving, she saw nothing more and decided all was clear and hopped into bed. Piling her hair on top of her head, she stuck a silk bonnet on and pulled the blankets clear up to her chin as she settled into her mound of pillows, hoping to get some well-needed rest.

Kinza dragged her feet forward, unable to stop. She walked through a dense jungle full of tall, twisting trees and ferns larger than she was. Yellow sunlight speckled through the treetops and almost reached the ground. Mist gathered low on the jungle floor, creeping around roots and grass.

She knew she had found it when she came upon it.

A totem pole staked into the ground in between two trees, well away from any path. The pole was a long branch, worn down, wrapped in beads, and topped by a skull with bright feathers surrounding the bone. Walking past it, she found the shimmering barrier rippling in the air. She pushed through, feeling only a slight pressure over her skin before it gave way.

Instead of being transported like she usually was, she continued to follow the path, her feet knowing the way. Vines and foliage dripped water onto her skin as she pushed past them until the jungle suddenly gave way and opened up to a large boulevard of shining silver stone. It was pristine and empty. She followed the road, looking up at the baobab trees that lined each side with perfect uniformity. They were smaller than normal, but still majestic and imposing. She couldn't see past the baobab trees as everything beyond was veiled in mist, but knew the boulevard bisected a great city. Her destination was in the center.

After walking for years and at the same time only moments, she reached the plaza in the middle. She was struck by the sheer size of the buildings immediately surrounding it. Tall, rectangular structures of glowing limestone encircled the plaza, palm trees placed at regular intervals, and a towering statue in the middle sat within a fountain. She couldn't get her eyes to focus on it, though.

Before she could take another step, warriors emerged from between the buildings. Every one of them was tall, with deep, glowing skin covered in white markings. The markings almost looked like tattoos, but older, more ancient. They all carried variations of obsidian weapons; swords, spears, scimitars, and daggers, each as beautiful as the night sky and wicked sharp. They moved, some of them quicker than she could see, with weapons raised and vengeful expressions. Terror suddenly exploded through Kinza, and one of the warriors stretched out an arm toward her, dark blade pointed right at her. Her abdomen burned lightening-hot as a white light erupted around her, throwing her attackers away like ragdolls to land on the silvery stone.

She screamed.

Kinza jolted awake, gasping for breath, sweat pouring down her face.

Something was wrong.

Her ears were ringing, so loud she could hardly focus on what was around her. Her eyes adjusted and looked upon her destroyed bedroom. Blinds ripped from the window, glass having shattered, papers and books scattered throughout the room, dust and debris floating in the air. But what she found beyond the end of her bed made her half-believe she was still dreaming. Her entire bedroom door, and the wall, was gone. The plaster, wood, and sheetrock were obliterated, and the remnants littered the living room floor across the hall. The house was still dark, so she could barely make anything out with just the moonlight to go by.

A pained groan came from beneath the rubble.

Grams! Kinza flew out of bed, blankets flying and bonnet falling off her head. She ran through her decimated bedroom, hopping over shards of glass to the sound.

"Kinza!" Grams' voice yelled in alarm. The sound was muffled but came from Grams' bedroom to the left down the hall. Then who was...

A too-large figure shifted under a section of wall, groaning again. Only then did she realize the voice was way too deep to be Grams'. Panic flooded her veins as she backed, panting, out of the room, down the hall to Grams' side. Kinza could see lights from the neighbor's house come on through the window.

Grams was struggling through a pile of blankets, eyes wide

and lips moving. Kinza's ears were still ringing, making it hard to comprehend what Grams was saying as she grabbed Kinza's arm. Thankfully she didn't look hurt, just alarmed.

"What?!" Kinza yelled. She tried to pull Grams to her feet, "We have to go! Someone is in the living room!"

Grams yanked her arm away from Kinza and gripped Kinza's face. The ringing was starting to subside. "Baby, you have to go!" Grams yelled in her face.

"I know, let's go!"

"No, sweetheart. They're here for you! You need to run." She started pushing Kinza away and scrambled to her night-stand, pulling something out of the top drawer.

"What? No! What are you talking about? There's a *man* in our *living room,* Grams!" She must not have realized what was happening. Kinza just had to get her out.

Grams had pulled out a small bit of cloudy stone, tied at the end of a cord, a crack running down the middle from inside a black velvet pouch. Kinza's head immediately started pound-ing, and she gripped her ears in pain. Grams covered the stone and held it to her breast, seemingly unaffected as Kinza was. As she covered the stone, the pain momentarily subsided. "Kinza, you listen to me *right now*, you hear me? You leave here imme-diately and run as far as you can. I'll hold him as long as I can, but baby, you've got to go. I'm so sorry. I thought they would never come back."

"Grams, what?!" Kinza truly felt she was still in a night-mare now. She reached for Grams' arm again, but the old lady shoved her away, eyes frantically pleading.

In the living room, pieces of the wall fell to the floor, and the figure struggled to get to their feet. A pounding knock came from the front door. Presumably, the neighbors checking out what the explosion was. She didn't dare run that way, though, as she would need to pass the man in the living room.

"Kinza, *GO NOW!*" Grams all but shrieked.

Kinza backed away, terrified by Grams' reaction, and stumbled to the hall and out the back door into the night. Running into the backyard, she looked around, unsure of where to go. It looked like the middle of the night. She could still see the moon high in the sky. She needed to hide and would come back later for Grams. She wouldn't go far. The neighbors to their right were standing in the backyard in bathrobes, yelling at her. She was too frantic to pay attention to what they were saying. She prayed they had already called the police.

She ran and hopped the back fence, the metal links digging into her thigh, and turned right to go down the alleyway that ran through the neighborhood. Her feet were pounding on the concrete, but she ignored the stinging for now. She sprinted to the end of the alley and crossed the street, and bolted through someone's yard, leaping over a bicycle and some children's toys. A dog was barking viciously from the yard next door.

A series of shouts came from behind her, and fear gripped her chest at the thought of Grams. She was too afraid of what the man would do to turn around and go back, though. So she kept running, hoping that she would lose him. She had gotten a pretty good head start.

Five minutes later, at the edge of her neighborhood, she paused, air wheezing in and out of her chest. *I am so not physically prepared for this,* she thought. She could see the outline of downtown in the distance but knew she couldn't run the whole way. There was another strip mall, a little larger than the other one, just a block away. She could hide in the alleyway until morning and then use one of the store's phones to call the police. She mentally cursed at herself for not grabbing her cellphone right away.

She started to run across the street and heard a fence clang a few houses behind her, much too loud to be a dog. Turning to look, icy fingers of terror seized her as she saw the large figure bounding over fences like a drunken hurdler at the Olympics. They were clearly injured, but the sheer size and ferocity of his movements horrified her. Kinza let out a little shriek and took off as fast as her feet would carry her. Tears started forming at the corners of her eyes, and she ran down the road, tipping over garbage cans behind her and scrambling over fences and across driveways. She could see the strip mall now, just across the next street, but the lights were still off. She hoped someone was in the parking lot, someone who could help her, but that hope was a dying thing.

Grunting came from behind her as the figure tripped over one of the garbage cans. Kinza wanted to cry, but the choking terror sent her feet into overdrive, slapping against the ground as she crossed the street, the building looming up in front of her.

A quick wind ruffled the ends of her hair as a shadow materialized before her, too fast to comprehend. Kinza didn't have time to scream as hands were on her and the world went dark.

CHAPTER 3
LUNATICS AND MADMEN

Zaid threw the body over his shoulder with ease and took off running down the street, muttering a string of curses.

This was *not* how this week should have gone.

He would be having a long discussion with Tahir when he got home. He had been stabbed, compelled, deceived, beaten, and outrun by ubir before, but they were all nearly identical situations. The same manic, unfocused restlessness behind their eyes, behavior barely checked. They couldn't go long without shedding blood; otherwise, their abilities would start to fade, and the healing would slow.

Never had he seen an ubir so calm and *human* before. He had come to the conclusion she had recently defected. There wasn't any other explanation.

The oddities just kept piling up. Was she also able to so completely compel the humans around her that they would defend her with a frying pan? The spot of his shoulder still ached where the old lady had whacked him. He was pretty sure it had been cast-iron. She also had a Deathstone. The searing pain in his head was unmistakable and nearly had him on his knees by the time the pan came swinging. Even after he smashed it, the after-effect had him vomiting in the yard and joints stiffening in pain.

Zaid had found no traces of any Auras in the house. No ubir, no Anunnaki, nothing. He had let himself in through the kitchen window, silently moving throughout the house, and entered the girl's room. She had been tossing and turning, sweat soaking the sheets. Now, *this* was more like a ubir. The sight had calmed him a little, ensuring everything wasn't as odd as it seemed. But the moment he had reached out to grab her, a force of radiant white light exploded from the bed, sending him crashing through the walls.

By the time he had steadied himself, she had gone. It had taken him almost ten minutes to subdue the old woman, avoid the neighbors, and catch back up to the girl. The old woman had moved faster than he would have expected, pulling the damn pan out from beneath her bed and wielding the Death-stone in the other. Even now, he still had spots flickering in his vision from the stone. He had put her in a hold, applied pressure on her neck at the right angles, and within moments her head had drooped.

As he moved through the streets with his mark over his shoulder, he headed back to the warehouse. It was only a few miles away, a little closer to downtown, but in a shadier neigh-borhood. When he first arrived, there had been a few people curled up in the corners, baring sparse yellow teeth at him, needles scattered around the floor. It only took him an hour to scare them away. He knew that they watched him from down the block and inside nearby houses used for the same purpose, waiting to see if he would leave again. He would soon.

The building itself was nondescript, two stories, but all the windows had fallen out with parts of the roof caving in. It looked as if it had been under construction at one point, but money had run out midway through. He pushed past the torn plastic hanging from the doorway and jogged up the stairs. He only had a small bag of things with him, not needing much. Dropping her in the corner of the room, he quickly bound her hands and feet with a few zip ties. Not that she could take him, but he also didn't know what her abilities were. If that white light was any indicator, he didn't want to find out.

As he sat down with his back to the wall, he finally got to see her up close and realized how young she looked, probably no more the seventeen or eighteen. He guessed she had been lured by older ubir with promises of power and the freedom to see the world instead of being cooped up in Rhapta. The younger ones were always easy to sway. He knew that better than anyone.

He looked over her prone form, noting the thick, black hair that fanned around her head. A few strands had fallen over her face. The delicate bridge of her nose between her eyes curved down to flare wider near the tip, which sat above full lips currently relaxed in sleep. Zaid admired her with the same blatant disregard he gave to most things.

When she didn't immediately stir, he leaned his head back against the wall, hoping to catch a bit of rest, not that he needed much.

It would be a long journey back to Rhapta.

KINZA WOKE to one particular beam of sunlight burning on the back of her eyelids, making her pounding headache way worse than it needed to be. She always closed her blinds before bed, so why was the sun coming through? Did she miss her alarm?

She peeled one eye open and struggled to reconcile the sight of the dilapidated concrete walls and dusty floor she was lying on.

"There's a bottle of water," came a deep voice with a rolling accent from across the room.

Kinza's eyes flew open at the memory of the night before, and she immediately bolted upright, the pain in her head throbbing harder. Across the room sat a man in black pants, a black hoodie, and black combat boots with his back to a wall. It was the man who blew up her house! Even from where she was, she could tell he would tower over her, one long leg stretched out before him. Muscled forearms fiddled with something in his lap. She had no idea how she ever thought she could outrun *that*. She had to get away. Why hadn't he killed her yet?

Kinza scrambled back, colliding with the wall behind her in a huff. "Who the hell are you?" she choked out, throat raw. "Screw that, HELP!" she screamed as best she could. "HELP! HEEEEEELPP!" she wailed toward the windows, keeping one eye on the man.

"*Stop* that," the man said, rolling his head in her direction. "There's no one around, so you're wasting your breath. Drink that," he said and jerked his chin at the water bottle before her. She realized he looked much younger than she had originally thought, maybe early twenties at best. Dark brown skin glowed in the strips of sunlight, and she could see a faint tattoo peeking out from his collar. He had a subtle scruff around his jaw as well, giving an I-haven't-shaved-in-a-few-days-but-I'm-too-unbothered type of vibe. In the back of her mind, she knew that if Mitra were here, she would have been making googly eyes at him. Something about him seemed oddly familiar to Kinza, though.

His lack of concern at kidnapping someone was starting to

piss her off. She had fully expected to be dead last night, but now, here she was tied up and he was just *sitting* there like they had just woken from a slumber party.

Not caring if it was poisoned, Kinza angrily grabbed the water bottle through her zip-tied hands and chugged it. It felt like sweet relief to her parched throat. She raised her arms over her head and hurtled the empty bottle at the man's head. He threw his arm up so fast it was a blur. She remembered the way he had moved the night before. "I *said,* who *the hell* are you?!" she shouted, much clearer now. She slammed her feet on the ground, trying to break the zip ties.

In the most nonchalant tone, he replied as if reciting, "My name is Zaid. I'm a *venari,* a bounty hunter from the Anunnaki tribe charged with capturing ubir like yourself. As my mark, I will take you back to Rhapta to face a trial for your crimes."

Kinza stopped. *Was this man mentally ill?* He must have been to attack an old lady and kidnap a young girl.

Grams! Tears pooled in her eyes as she gritted her teeth. "What did you do to my grandma? What did you do?" She almost didn't want to know the response. She couldn't bear it.

Zaid gave a disgusted expression and snorted. "Drop the act. You're the one who compelled her to attack me with a frying pan. Either way, I put her to sleep and left her at that house," he said, waving a hand in a vague direction, eyes closed. And then, as an afterthought, "I don't kill humans."

His response bewildered Kinza. What was he talking about? He seriously must be some sort of psychopath, and the thought of being around such an unhinged lunatic brought a twisting sense of fear back to her chest. "You listen to me right now," she said in a voice as deadly as sin. It was the same voice her mother had used when Kinza had crossed a line during backtalk. "You are going to cut these stupid ties, and then you are going to let me walk out of here, and you are *never* going to come around my family and me again. Do. You. Understand. Me?"

Zaid just snorted again and fiddled with the thing in his lap. She could finally see what it was, a wicked-looking obsidian dagger. The hilt looked like it was made of gold and wrapped in leather.

Obsidian!

The memory of the warriors in her nightmare came hurtling back. The man before her looked just like them, albeit in normal clothes and sans warpaint. "Look," he said, opening his eyes. "I don't know what kind of game you're playing, but if you could be silent the rest of the way there, I would highly appreciate that."

"Rest of the way there? Where are you taking me?" So this maniac wasn't going to immediately kill her? Kinza's mind started spiraling down into a dark place.

"As I *just* told you," he said as if to a child. "We are going back to Rhapta, where you are going to stand trial for your crimes, as all ubir do." He pointed the blade at her during the last remark.

"Ubir what? Where the hell is Rhapta? Mexico?" She struggled against the zip ties again, but the man was clearly unconcerned over her efforts, not even looking up. She let out another shriek of frustration.

He rolled his eyes, getting up. "We leave in a few hours. Feel free to rest until then." He turned and walked to a duffel bag on the opposite side of the room, grabbed something out of it, and headed down a decaying staircase in the center of the floor.

Kinza tried rolling to her feet, eyeing the duffel bag. Maybe there was something sharp inside she could use to cut herself free. Regardless, based on the view from the window, she was on the second floor and didn't think she could jump out the window without twisting her ankle or breaking her back.

"Don't bother," Zaid's voice came from downstairs. "I'll know the moment you move."

Kinza flopped back to the floor, reality setting in. This man was seriously crazy and intended to bring her to wherever the heck Rhapta was. She had no idea what he was talking about. He made literally no sense.

Tears welled in her eyes again, and she didn't bother stopping them this time. There were always those crime shows on tv, with the evil murderers in ski masks and the innocents they kidnapped. By the time each episode started, the victim was already dead, and yeah, it was sad. But no one ever talked about the time in between, while the victim was waiting to die, helpless and not knowing if that day was their last. She couldn't handle the suspense of not knowing what would happen next.

She took a deep breath in, and then out, and then in again. She would *not* be a helpless little lamb. If this psychopath intended to kill her, she would go out swinging. She heard his footsteps downstairs, walking through the rubble of the building. The steps echoed and eventually faded, maybe even leaving.

Looking around for something close to her, she noted a sharp rock under a pile of dust and plaster. She leaned over ever so quietly and stretched her arms as far as she could toward the rock. Snagging the corner, she pulled it closer, the edge scraping on the floor.

She froze and waited to see if the man, Zaid, would come running back up the stairs, but the room remained silent. Picking up the piece, she brought it close and tucked it between her palms, using the zip-tie to wedge it in tightly. Once she was satisfied, she bent her knees to either side, stretching the tie around her legs as best she could. Raising her arms over her head again, she sucked in a breath and slammed the rock down.

She could hear the distant sound of traffic, but no murderers came rushing up the stairs.

Looking down, she saw she only grazed the tie; it didn't break. It took fifteen minutes and several attempts to free her ankles. Her hands were raw and bleeding by the time she was done. But a trickle of pride swelled at the sight of her freed legs. She moved to start on her wrists, but the faintest scrape of a shoe on concrete came from outside the window.

She whipped around and hunched against the wall away from the staircase, pretending she was crying. She heard Zaid's solid footsteps come up the stairs and a rustle of fabric. Her heart started beating frantically in her chest.

Zaid froze on the other side of the room. "I told you I'm just taking you to your trial. I'm not going to kill you." She could hear him come closer and toss a pile of what looked like clothing and a pair of shoes at her feet. She had forgotten that all she was wearing were men's boxer shorts and an oversized t-shirt. Where had he gotten that so fast? There weren't any shopping malls nearby. She didn't have time to be self-conscious, though, and gripped the rock securely, waiting for the right moment.

When she didn't answer, Zaid came closer.

His hand clamped down on her shoulder, and she struck. The grunt that came out of him was almost as satisfying as the impact the rock made on his cheekbone, a large gash appearing. He stumbled to the ground, catching himself on a knee, one hand going to his cheek. Violent rage flashed in his eyes.

Kinza wasted no time getting to her feet and hurtled across the room and all but fell down the stairs, hands still tied. As she got to the bottom step, she heard a scraping sound upstairs and knew she was dead. Impossibly fast, a moment later, arms locked around her chest, pinning her biceps to her sides. She threw her head back as hard as she could and heard a loud crunch. The man just let out a frustrated growl and lifted her up, her feet well above the ground now. She started kicking and flailing in the air as hard as she could.

She would *not* die like this. The image of her mother's limp hand came unbidden to her mind.

"Heelpp!" she screamed. "Someone, please help me!" she screamed and sobbed, her throat going raw again. She couldn't get a purchase as she tried scraping and clawing at him.

"Stop!" Zaid yelled, his deep voice rumbling against her back. He stumbled backward and sat down toward the bottom of the stairs, wrapping his calves around Kinza's and lifting his chin so she couldn't headbutt him again.

She thrashed, again and again, gaining no traction. It was like trying to lift a horse off her, and she eventually stopped, tears tracking down her face.

"Are you done yet?" Zaid asked.

Kinza just let out another scream in response.

"Fine. I can sit here all day, but you can make this easier for both of us."

She didn't reply and just sat there, feeling defeated. After close to ten breaths, Zaid released his hold a fraction of an inch, but no more. "Why?" she mumbled, more to herself than anyone. "What did I do?" The tears wouldn't stop now that they had started. Fury had quickly disintegrated into hopelessness.

"I've told you probably four times now. Ubir go to Rhapta for their trials. Blood magic is illegal and dangerous."

"I have no idea what you are talking about, you *lunatic*," she sobbed. "I don't know what a ubir is or where Rhapta is, and I sure as hell don't play any magic games." She sniffled a bit. "I think you have the wrong girl."

Zaid was silent for a moment. "Your name is Kinza Solace, is it not?"

Tears dribbled down her face, but she nodded.

"Then you are wanted for being a ubir. It's possible your parents made you complete the blood rite when you were a child, but you can explain that at your trial. It happens sometimes."

Kinza craned her head to the side, trying to look at him, but all she could see was the sleeve of his shirt. "Dude. Bro. Sir. My parents are *dead*. My mom was a dental assistant, and my dad was in sales. That was it. I've never heard of any of the things you are talking about."

"I don't know what to tell you. It's my job to bring you in, and you can defend yourself at the trial."

"And what happens if I'm found guilty at this trial thing? Do they still let me go home?"

Zaid hesitated. "No... everyone found guilty is sentenced to death." It sounded so final, so absolute.

Silent tears kept falling down Kinza's face, and she nodded as if in acceptance. "Okay, then," she said quietly. She was too tired to keep fighting.

"If I let go, will you stay calm?" Zaid asked.

Kinza gave another small nod. He released her a moment later, pausing to see if she would flail like a rabid animal again. But she just sat there. "What now?" she asked.

"You can go upstairs and change into the clothes I brought you." He reached out and hesitantly cut the zip ties around her wrists.

"Ah. We want the inmate to look presentable," she said sarcastically. "Makes sense." Without looking at him, she trudged back up the stairs.

ZAID WATCHED the girl walk up the stairs. His cheek throbbed from the gash and his nose, but he knew it was already healing, the skin knitting back together. While she was quiet now, he didn't think she would continue this sullen attitude the whole way there. It was only a matter of time until the volcano of rage erupted again. He reached a hand up to his nose.

Yup. Definitely broken.

On an inhale, he cracked it back into place, waves of pain flowing through his face, but he ignored it. After a few moments, he could feel the warm, prickling sensation of the healing as it began again.

He needed to find a way to keep her calm until they got there. Then he would deposit her into the Elders' waiting cells and would wash his hands of her and maybe take a nice vacation or something. He hadn't been to Tahiti in a while.

Zaid climbed the crumbling stairs when he no longer heard the rustle of clothing. When he got up there, she was dressed and sitting with her back to the wall, forearms resting on her knees. She looked up at him, "If I can't convince you that I'm not an ubir or whatever, then how can I convince a bunch of judges? Is there even a jury?"

He heaved a breath and sat on an open windowsill, the breeze coming through nicely. He just looked at her and shrugged, trying not to exacerbate her mood.

"Can we play a game?" she asked.

"A game?" he asked incredulously.

"Yeah," she wiped at the drying tears on her face. "I will answer a question for every question you answer for me."

Zaid thought for a moment. The answers to the questions he guessed she wanted would be of no consequence. The only part of his job that was secretive was keeping tribal matters out of human knowledge. He didn't do overly well at that last part the night before, with the whole neighborhood waking up, but it would be fine. The Ummanu would take care of it. In the meantime, though, he could try to find out what her abilities were. He still had no idea what that wave of white light energy had been back at the house. Maybe it was a new ability? This could be his way to find out.

"Okay," he said with a nod.

She looked a smidge brighter at the agreement. "Okay, um. Where are you taking me?"

"Rhapta," he said, not for the first time.

"Okay, but where is that?"

"Tanzania, south of Mount Kilimanjaro, but also on another plane of existence, in a way. It's here, but only Anunnaki can get there." She furrowed her brow but looked at him expectantly. "Ah, what are your abilities?"

She just blinked at him. "I can juggle and wiggle my ears, and I've never lost a game of Mario Kart. Well, okay, maybe just a few times. Um, what is an ubir?"

He folded his arms. "An ubir is an Anunnaki that has broken from the collective Aura by using blood magic, usually through a blood rite sacrifice." Her face twisted in disgust. "How old are you?"

"Eighteen. How old are you?"

Zaid paused for a moment, not anticipating any personal questions. "Twenty-one. Tell me about your parents."

She scowled. "That's not the same kind of question."

He didn't respond, just looked at her and awaited her answer.

She huffed a breath. "I told you. My mom was a dental hygienist born in Chicago and met my dad, who was in sales, at a party the summer after high school. They were together ever since, basically best friends." She looked away, drawn into her own thoughts for a moment. "They died when I was nine. What's an Anunnaki?"

"We are an ancient tribe, older than the oldest civilization. Anunnaki have existed all throughout human history, and we have several myths on how we came to be, but none of them are the same. Humans have noted our existence, but we try to keep that from happening, so we end up as stories they tell by the fire. Think Mesopotamian gods, Tuatha de Danann of Ireland, angels of the Bible. Anunnaki are stronger and heal faster, live longer than humans, in addition to the... gifts that we each have. While we may look human, we are different. We live in Rhapta as a guiding hand to humanity, albeit from inside the city. We cannot leave. It would cause too much chaos in the world. How did they die?"

She looked up at him under lowered eyelids. "You did not just call yourself a god. And pick a different question."

Zaid looked toward the ceiling as if to roll his eyes. "What did you attack me with back at the house?"

Now Kinza looked truthfully confused. "Me? Attack you? You came into my house, remember? And you blew up *my* room. It's not my fault you screwed it up." She picked at a seam on the green cargo pants he had brought her.

"Do you not remember the white light? And I didn't blow anything up. It's not one of my abilities."

Her dark eyes snapped up. "Abilities? What does that actually mean? Like what?"

"It's my turn still. You really have no idea what that light was?"

She shook her head, eyebrows lowered. "I remember having a nightmare, and then I woke up, and my room was destroyed, and some freak was in my living room." She raised an eyebrow at him. The sheer level of sass that emanated out of her every pore must have been an ability on its own. "Okay, my turn. What are your 'abilities?'" she asked.

Zaid sighed. "Besides Anunnaki passive abilities, I can move at the speed of sound, and I can sense heartbeats up to a quarter-mile radius. Why did the old lady have a Deathstone?"

"Uh-huh....and I have no idea what that is."

Zaid was becoming frustrated by her lack of knowledge. "Okay, where is your tribal marker?"

Her face was a chagrined question mark.

"Your tattoo, where is it?" Shock registered across her face, and her eyes narrowed.

"You watched me change! You perv!"

"No, all Anunnaki have them. So you *do* have one then?"

She hesitated a moment before saying, "For as long as I can remember, I've had a tattoo. I have no idea where I got it." She waited another moment before lifting the light blue tank top to reveal the tattoo on her upper abdomen. Zaid froze, the circular symbol of the tribe was there, but there was more to the tattoo. Tiny chains and what looked like gemstones extended out both sides in an intricate design. He had never seen one like that.

His was larger than normal, but that was due to the *venari* pact; they all had it when they accepted the job. It allowed him to keep his abilities when he left the city, but only for a month at a time. There were limits, of course.

"Ah. So there we go," he said, not elaborating on the tattoo's oddness. "You're Anunnaki. Case closed. Now, as fun as this game has been, we have to get going soon. Are you going to behave yourself, or do I need to tie you up again?"

She inhaled so fast at the threat he thought she was about to pounce, a scowl twisted her face into rage. Honestly, the speed at which her emotions could change would put a typhoon to shame. It was almost glorious. But she clicked her teeth shut and said, "So I still have to go with you?"

He nodded.

She looked down. "Okay, I won't tear your face off on three conditions. One, we get to keep playing. Two, you never knock me out again like you did last night. And three, we gotta stop at Walgreens or something. I'm starving, my hair is a disaster, I have a migraine, and I really need some Chapstick."

Zaid just grunted in confirmation. He did not expect her to keep to that agreement in the slightest. "Meet me downstairs in five minutes."

CHAPTER 4

A BITTERSWEET BOON

TEN YEARS AGO

Zaid stood at the edge of the practice ring, watching the older boys attempt every possible maneuver to take each other to the ground. The soft sand did little to cushion the falls, but still more so than dull bone swords that they cracked against their skinny arms.

Zaid ran along the length of the gate, trying to keep up with them and see through the slats. His breath came quickly, but he grinned the whole time anyway. The practice ring and the barracks surrounding them sat on the north side of the city in a tight cluster of limestone. It housed the military as well as the younger pupils who had yet to receive the red markings of a full warrior.

As he ran along watching the pupils practice, Zaid imagined himself, a few years older and training along with them, swinging massive, ridged bone swords and walking through the city in markings of red paint. People would look on in awe as he passed by, and his mother and brother would smile as he came home and praise him—

A slight hand fell onto his shoulder, effectively startling him out of his daydream.

What are you doing here, little brother? Amir stood behind him, blocking out the sun that attempted to blind Zaid. He had to shield his eyes against the halo shining around his brother.

Just watching, Zaid said sheepishly. In truth, only pupils were supposed to be in the training grounds, and Zaid was most certainly not a pupil. At eleven years old, he had not manifested any of his abilities yet, which was a year later than normal. Most children manifested during their tenth year, and his latency was the sole point of scrutiny of his classmates.

Amir had manifested by the time he was nine, something almost unheard of. And his ability to calm even the most frazzled of demeanors was something their mother cherished in her constant worry over her youngest son. Amir's ability was a bit broader than that; he could feel the emotions of those around him. So far, he hadn't been able to influence any of those emotions other than as a calming balm, but that was enough. *Better to be gentle than do something you'd regret,* their mother would say.

Come, you are not supposed to be here, Amir said, attempting to be stern. But at fifteen, he had a hard time keeping the slight smile from his face when his little brother was around, even if he was rarely around anymore to see him.

When they were younger, they had been much closer. Their father had died when Zaid was a baby, but their mother did just fine on her own. At least from their eyes. They would run through the city barefoot and steal fruit from vendors on the main road. They would climb the baobab trees and the Aurastones and swim in the warm, clear pools of water in the plazas.

Of course, it never took long for the guards to chase them away.

It was on one such excursion that Zaid had decided he wanted to be in the warrior class. As he and Amir were running away from a menacing-looking guard with an obsidian-tipped spear, they collided with a wall of muscle and fell to the ground. Looking up, they found a giant of a man. At nearly seven feet tall, the warrior looked like a chiseled god from mythology. The red warpaint markings swirled over his chest and biceps in intricate patterns.

There weren't nearly as many warriors as one would think, though. From his studies, Zaid knew that the Anunnaki population was dwindling, and the city that could hold millions only housed a few hundred thousand now. The warrior class was difficult to move into as well. One needed to have abilities that were useful to the military as well as a tough state of mind. Everyone knew how hard it was to become a pupil, so when the warriors in red paint strode through the city, everyone stopped in awe. Very similarly to Amir and Zaid at that moment.

The warrior had scolded them and told them not to climb the Aurastones anymore, but all Zaid remembered was the look on the faces of those around them. The guard who had been chasing them had stopped and bowed his head in respect. A vendor across the street stopped his shouting, and a woman carrying a child had paused to stare as well. Zaid wanted someone to look at him the same way they looked at the warrior now. Like he *was* someone.

As soon as Amir was old enough, he started to fill the fatherly role that was absent in their lives. Well, at least he tried. Their mother worked as a tailor at the edge of the city, the furthest you could go while still being in the psychic barrier. Any further, and you would be in the slums, not that he would mind living there. It was more interesting anyway. But they had just enough from her work to eat and retain their house. Amir became ambitious, though, wanting to make more money and increase their standing enough to move to one of the more central plazas. All the houses there were massive.

Amir started to spend more time away from home meeting with people he swore could help them, and soon they would be swimming in shillings, and Mother could wear the finest fabrics. The irony was that Mother had no intention of leaving. She had married their father and spent the beginning of their lives in their little home. It was small but bright and not too close to the training grounds that permanently smelled of sweat.

As Amir steered Zaid away from the training grounds and back toward one of the long boulevards that ran through the city, he kept a hand on his shoulder. The steady calm that emanated from his brother's hand was grounding after watching the fighting pupils. They stopped at a vendor, and Amir bought them a few *guakal,* fist-sized, ridge-shelled, lime-green fruits with little red spikes on the outside. Once broken into, Zaid sank his teeth into the sweet flesh of the interior of the *guakal.*

They sat on the edge of the street in the shade of a baobab and watched throngs of people moving along. Merchants called out wares, miners returning from the Aurastone quarries, and scholars in blue paints moved about in groups. From where they sat, they could see the top of the Grand Hall poking about a set of buildings in the center of the city. Zaid knew that the Elders resided in the hall and never left, but his best friend Khalil had sworn he had seen one walking down an adjects street just the night before. Zaid had laughed at him.

Suddenly people started muttering and moving to the sides of the street, sending glares or furtive glances toward the man walking through. Zaid had to stand up to see who it was and almost dropped his *guakal.*

A short man walked down the center of the boulevard in human clothes. And if the clothes didn't give it away, he could see the man's mark on his right arm. It looked the same as everyone else's, a mandala with a pair of eyes in the center, but it extended out in all directions, the edges of the mandala twisting out further was an abundance of detail to cover the majority of his arm.

Venari. They were the only ones with marks like that and the only ones who wore the stiff, dull fabric of human clothes.

As the man moved past where they were sitting, people pushed to get away from them. The *venari* were few in number, fewer than they had ever been. Their unusual tattoos and connection to the human world made them... dirty in the minds of Rhaptans. They kept to themselves and only returned between missions, which were frequent. No one knew exactly how one became *venari*, but Kahlil had told Zaid once that if you had an ability they were interested in, they would show up at your doorstep and take you away right then and there. They very rarely let anyone opt out of it; you needed to have pretty extreme extenuating circumstances or a pardon from one of the Elders themselves.

If you were taken, your family would start to receive similar treatment of being considered unlucky. Zaid knew that the job was important. Many ubir went out and caused havoc in the human world, threatening Rhapta's precarious position, but the stigma that came with being *venari* was almost as unappealing.

Zaid watched the man's retreating back and prayed for a warrior's ability.

A FEW WEEKS LATER, Zaid crept around the back of the barracks, keeping an eye out for any trainers that might kick him out again.

It was the only day of the week he didn't have school. All children in Rhapta attended six days a week until they were fifteen. At that point, they could either continue on their studies to become a scholar or begin an apprenticeship. It was at that time that many young boys attempted to showcase their abilities in the warrior's training grounds, hoping to be picked as a pupil. It was nearing the end of the school year with a month-long reprieve soon, and many boys were doing just that right now.

Zaid just wanted to take a look. It wouldn't hurt anybody. Just a peek.

A crowd was forming around one of the training rings while trainers stood just inside, barking orders at a pair of teenage boys sparring in the ring. As Zaid wiggled his way through the mass of people, he could see flashes of light followed by a ripple of laughter through the crowd. It was rare to hear that much sound in this part of the city. People generally only spoke through Auras and left the verbal speech to the slums. He finally burst through to the front and saw what everyone was laughing at.

A gangly boy was trying to showcase his ability to the older warriors, but unfortunately, it looked like all he was doing was flashing sparks of light in his opponent's face as he got close. It did nothing more than momentarily distract his opponent.

The opponent, on the other hand, grinned before the colors of his skin shifted, and he vanished. It was Feroz. The crowd gasped and clapped. Feroz was one of several older boys who frequently got Zaid in trouble. They liked to humiliate him by reminding him of the fact he hadn't gotten his ability yet. Zaid hoped he lost but wasn't expecting it.

The first boy spun around looking for Feroz, and Zaid could see a ripple on the ground.

He wasn't exactly invisible, just shifting the colors around him like camouflage. The first boy suddenly grunted and fell to the ground clutching his stomach. He had lost.

Feroz came back into view, raising a fist in the air in triumph. The crowd cheered again. There was no doubt he would be picked to train as a pupil.

Zaid moved back, trying to get out of view before Feroz saw him. If he did—

Zaid Hatem! a voice called. He half debated making a run for it, but the crowd turned to look at where Feroz was pointing, which happened to be right at Zaid. *Master,* Feroz said, looking toward the nearest trainer. *It looks like little Zaid would like to demonstrate his abilities.* A few people who knew about Zaid's....condition laughed.

The trainer walked into view. It was Maheer, a stocky man with his hair shorn close to his head. Zaid knew his hands were covered in scars from years of training with the obsidian weapons. Those hands had frequently thrown him out of the training grounds.

Maheer nodded in agreement. *Hatem,* he said. *If you spend so much of your time here, you must have something to show us.* Feroz grinned wickedly behind him. *Get in here, and you will spar with... Parwez.*

Zaid internally groaned. This was going to hurt. He walked back to the ring and climbed over the bars as Parwez did the same from the other side. Not only was Parwez five years older than him, but his ability was also strength. Once, several years ago, Zaid had witnessed him punch through the branch of a baobab on a dare. The entire branch had broken off and fallen to the ground in a loud crash. One could only imagine what that would have done to a person.

Zaid's heart started beating frantically as the other boy came closer. He was of average build, but of course, that was deceptive. His hair was kept in short twists about his head, and he narrowed his eyes as Zaid stopped in the middle of the ring. The soft sand shifted under Zaid's feet, and his palms started to sweat. This was really going to hurt.

Maheer whistled for them to begin.

Zaid tried to think fast as Parwez started running toward him, but fear had his mind going blank. Parwez got close and raised his fist, and swung. Zaid threw himself to the left, a knuckle just barely grazing his cheek.

Parwez turned and threw another punch aimed at his gut, but Zaid instinctively shifted to the right. The lack of impact had Parwez stumbling, and Zaid almost smiled, but his heart was still pounding, and all his focus was on not getting hit.

Parwez stood, this time anger twisted at his features. He knew the trainers were watching, and while it was unlikely he would be expelled as a pupil, he didn't want his reputation tarnished by a little boy with no abilities. So he settled into a stance, and Zaid was frozen in place again. Parwez dashed two steps forward, twisted, and rocketed his arm at Zaid's face.

Zaid could almost hear the collective satisfaction through the collective Auras of the crowd, knowing he couldn't dodge this hit, Parwez was too close this time, and Zaid had waited too long to move.

In a blink, Zaid had reacted on some primal instinct again and sidestepped. As he was moving, he watched in slow motion as Parwaz's fist soared right by him, and as soon as Zaid stopped moving, things sped up again.

The crowd gasped. Zaid didn't understand what had happened.

Parwez stumbled and fell to the ground. He whirled and got to his feet, looking at Zaid incredulously. In a fury, he came at him again. This time Zaid ran several steps to the right at the last possible second. He watched again as he moved; Parwez swung in slow motion until Zaid stopped several feet away.

The mental chatter from the crowd was getting louder. But Zaid kept up this dance. Parwez would come at him, swing, and by the time he finished, Zaid would be standing several feet away, having moved too fast for Parwez to strike.

After several minutes of this, Maheer called out, *Enough!* Both boys stopped. Parwez bent over, hands on his knees, and panted. He looked up through his hair and glared at Zaid, who was barely winded.

Zaid looked around at the dumbstruck faces of the crowd and Maheer and Feroz's confused expressions. Was this... was this his ability? Had it finally manifested? *What is this?* Maheer snapped. When Zaid didn't immediately reply, he stalked over to him and moved to clamp a hand on his shoulder.

Zaid ran. The world moved slowly again as he ran to the far edge of the training ground, hopped the fence, and kept running until he was out of the warrior's grounds and down to the main boulevard that ran through the center of town. He kept running until he was in the western quarter, which was nearly empty.

Rhapta's dwindling population meant that large sections of the city were uninhabited. The city was built to house many more, but with the increasing emigration into the human world, through ubir or transitions into human society, areas such as the western quarter started to decay.

The large limestone buildings towered several stories high. Rhaptan architecture had a uniformity to it. Long, rectangular buildings with high windows and high ceilings kept out the heat of the African sun. The baobab trees were the only vegetation in the more inhabited areas, but in the western quarter, vines, moss, and little flowers crept back over buildings and through doorways. Cracks started forming in the limestone as nature started taking back its home.

It was in one of these buildings that Zaid finally stopped running, and the world sped up again. He was out of breath now and sat down against a wall covered in moss. It was soft, and the building was cool. Dropping his head down to his knees, he fell asleep.

Zaid woke to the sound of thunder rumbling across the city. It was much darker, almost twilight, and a gentle rain came down outside of the building. The wall adjacent to him had partially crumbled, and vines covered part of the opening, leaving him a scattered view of a small plaza beyond.

He sighed, realizing he had missed dinner and his mother would be angry. The happy news of his manifested ability should have been enough to have him running home to joyfully tell her, but instead, the knowledge of his ability sat like a stone in the pit of his stomach.

Why wasn't he happier? He could move faster than anyone could catch! That was better than anything he could have hoped for. And surely it was more than enough to get a spot as a warrior's pupil? Maybe it was the fact that no one had cheered for him when he won? No one had smiled or stared in awe. They had only looked on in dumbstruck confusion. As if they wondered how *he* could get such an ability. That wasn't what he wanted.

Zaid heard a faint sound coming from the plaza. It was steady as a drumbeat and in perfect rhythm. He cocked his head and listened as it got closer, and a few moments later, Amir pushed his way through the vines, startling him and the steady beat faded away.

Hello, little brother. I see I have found you, Amir said not ungently. He sat down next to Zaid, who put his head back on his knees. *I heard what happened. Congratulations!* Zaid didn't know what to say, so Amir put his hand on the back of his neck, and Zaid slowly started to release the tension he didn't realize he was holding.

After a few minutes in silence, Zaid said, *is Mother angry that I missed dinner?*

Mmm, no. She was overjoyed to hear you manifested your ability, but saddened when you did not come home to tell her. Why did you run?

I don't know...

Do you not like your ability? Or were you just testing it? he teased. Amir tried to keep a balance between being a wise older brother and the laughter-filled boy he had been when he was younger.

No, I do like it. It's just... He picked his head up. *It's not what I expected.*

Ah, Amir said, understanding. *You thought people would love you and fawn over you the moment it manifested then?*

Zaid shrugged.

Amir gripped his shoulders. *You must understand, people aren't in awe of the powerful. They are in awe of those they* perceive *are powerful. Things like money, status, and reputation are what they look for. That is how the Elders got to their position; they played their cards at just the right time, knowing when to play the card that will wow the crowd most.* Amir leaned down to look at him and gave him a little shake. *Don't you worry, little brother, we will get there. I promise.*

Zaid didn't understand what he meant, not truly. But his brother's calming presence seemed to repair his tarnished mood, and he smiled a little. Amir gave him a smile twice as big. Zaid would miss that smile soon. Amir had accepted an apprenticeship the week prior. He was going to start studying with the scholars. In truth, the branch he was to apprentice under was more focused on aiding the Elders than pure scholarly research, but that was what he wanted.

Come, Amir said, *let's go home before Mother comes looking for us.*

LATER THAT EVENING, Zaid sat in the main room of their small home after dinner. His mother had been angry that he and Amir had come home sopping wet but gave him a kiss on each cheek afterward to say he was blessed to have received such an ability that day.

She had given him a bit of food and told him not to be late the next day. Afterward, they sat together in the main room and relaxed while the rain continued to pour outside. In this area of the city, at the edge but not outside the psychic barrier of the collective Aura, there were multitudes of apartments stacked side by side or on top of each other, limestone overlapping. Stairs twisted around outside and separated the homes, and they all surrounded small courtyards and alleys where people would hang bright strips of cloth and beads from balcony to balcony.

He had often wondered why they had to live so closely together when much of the city lay empty. Most of the central plazas were already occupied, but many other homes were abandoned and available for use. Amir told him it was because the Elders had decreed that they must remain empty. He had used this as another lesson to point out that the Elders did this as a display of power. As long as it was flaunted in such a manner, people would believe them powerful and would continue to obey. Zaid didn't understand that either, but he didn't actually care. He liked their home.

It was small but beautiful. From their home at the top of a cluster of apartments, Zaid could see the tops of a line on baobab trees a street over through the open window. The air was humid, but his mother said the cleansing properties of water were good for the home. Every time it stormed, she would keep the shutters open as long as possible to let the mist coming off the rain make its way into the house.

She sat in the corner on a low cushion covered in a pile of furs. He knew his mother was beautiful. The other women said so. Short, dense coils sat about her head above a wide forehead and deep, glowing skin. Amir got his build from her, both of them slight but quick like a gazelle. It was ironic that he was the one who had ended up with the speed ability.

Amir sat in another corner, reading by candlelight, studying for his upcoming apprenticeship, and Zaid lounged on a stack of blankets against the opposite wall, listening to the rain. He had school tomorrow and thought about how his classmates would react once they found out about his ability.

As he lay there, Zaid started to hear a faint sound as he had earlier. It was similar in rhythm, but as it got louder, he realized it sounded more like three separate drums beating out of sync, each keeping to its own rhythm.

He sat up and cocked his head, trying to hear better.

His mother looked over at him. *What is it, my love?* she asked, smiling faintly.

Zaid's eyebrows pinched together, and he shook his head. The sounds were getting louder and something like fear prickled across his skin. What was it? Amir had stopped reading and looked at him as well. As the sound got closer, his mother whipped her head to the door, and Zaid could hear footsteps outside.

Zaid, get— his mother started to shout, rising from her seat, but before she could finish, the door burst open. Two men strode in and stood to the side, followed by a third man who was tall and wiry. He moved with precision, standing straight-backed with hands crossed behind him.

Who are you? Zaid's mother shouted. *What are you doing in my home?*

The third man spoke. *Good evening. My name is Savar Basu, and I'm the head venari trainer.* He gave a slight nod in greeting.

No... Zaid's mother said, looking at her son. *You cannot... it is too dangerous for him!*

Unfortunately, the number of ubir is increasing, and we need every possible Anunnaki we can take. It has been decided.

No! she shouted and lurched toward Zaid, who didn't fully comprehend what was happening. The two other men strode across the room to hold her back while keeping an eye on Amir, who stood scowling and silent in the corner. Zaid could have sworn he felt the rage emanating off his brother, but was too distracted by Savar to know.

Savar came over toward Zaid, who stood and looked to the door. Just as he was about to run, Savar pulled a small cloudy stone from his pocket. It had a crack down the middle and hung from a piece of cord.

Deathstone.

Zaid, Amir, and their mother all suddenly clamped their hands to their heads, screaming through gritted teeth. A high-pitched whine permeated the room, and Zaid felt as if his head would split open. Savar came forward and tied a bit of pale rope about one wrist and put the stone back in his pocket. The pain receded. Only then did Zaid notice the three men had something stuffed in their ears keeping them from being susceptible to the Deathstone's song.

As soon as the pain receded, he tried to run, but Savar easily caught him. Zaid realized the rope must have been *laqueus,* used to bind and dampen abilities. While it was around his wrist, he could only run at the speed of a regular eleven-year-old.

Savar pushed him against the wall, and he heard his mother yelling again. Savar took out a small, blue Aurastone, small enough it would fit in Zaid's palm, and pressed it against the tattoo on his chest. Savar closed his eyes and mumbled a few words. The stone became hot, and just as he was about to yell, it was removed.

His mother had stopped shouting and looked at his tattoo with sorrow. It had grown! Zaid saw that the outer ring of the tattoo extended just slightly further than it had before. It wasn't much, but any Anunnaki would know what it meant.

He had been tapped as *venari.*

CHAPTER 5

FEVER DREAMS OF CLARITY

Kinza did not plan on keeping to the agreement in the slightest. She clearly wasn't going to muscle her way out of Zaid's grip, but maybe she could sneak away somehow. She couldn't lie to herself either. The things he said about the tribal mark and how he knew she had that tattoo had rattled her a little. Everything he had said prior to that could be explained away by drugs or psychosis, but that little bit of information had stuck with her. While looking for a way to escape, she could see if he truly knew anything about it in the meantime. He might as well be useful.

The sun was on its downward arc, and Kinza could tell it was close to rush hour based on the sound of the traffic coming from the highway. Her stomach grumbled, confirming the time. She hadn't eaten since the night before, and she was starting to feel light-headed. Looking down at her hands, she saw that the cuts on her palms from the rock weren't as bad as she originally thought. They were already scabbed over.

After agreeing for the seventeenth time that she wouldn't

start screaming again, Zaid led her out of the building and down the street. Looking around, she guessed she was a good mile from her house. The warehouse was definitely in a neighborhood where she wouldn't walk at night, and she hoped they would leave soon. Zaid said nothing as he walked to a car on the side of the road and, in broad daylight, slammed his elbow into the back window.

"Yes, please keep making that much noise. Maybe someone will hear you and rescue me."

Zaid just gave her a tolerant look and hot-wired the car in under a minute. Sliding into the driver's seat, he said, "Get in." She didn't know why she expected less of a kidnapper.

Looking around one more time, Kinza rushed over to the passenger's side and climbed in. The car was clearly as old as she was and looked like a dump. Fast food bags and paper cups littered the floor. A few articles of rancid clothing were in the back, making her roll down the window for a single breath of fresh air.

They sat in silence for the first few minutes before Kinza pointed out a drugstore on the corner.

"We can stop somewhere out of town. I'm not stupid enough to stop so close to where you live," Zaid said. He had moved the seat back as far as it would go, but he still looked like an elephant crammed into a clown car. So this wasn't his first rodeo. Great.

She just rolled her eyes to the ceiling and stared out the window, watching as they entered and eventually exited the horrible Chicago traffic. The city slowly drifted by as they got further and further out of town. She realized that Grams and Mitra would be worried sick about her. Her professors must have thought she skipped class, and Karin would probably count this against her somehow when she got back.

If she got back.

"How are we getting to Tanzania? The airport is the opposite direction," she asked after a while.

"I don't use airports. We are headed to upstate Michigan, on the east side of the lake. A friend of mine has a portal there we can use," he replied. Kinza gave him a deadpan look and turned back to the window. She had to admire the sheer level of commitment he had to his fantasy world.

"Oh, yes. Of course," she said, overly agreeable. "A portal. How could I have been so silly?"

Zaid drove for another thirty minutes before pulling into the parking lot of a drug store. Usually, by now, he would have had his mark bound and gagged in the trunk, but he wanted to ask the girl, Kinza, more questions. From the start, everything about this mission had gone totally sideways, and he was starting to wonder if he had been given the wrong name.

But she has the tattoo, he thought to himself. The only Anunnaki outside of Rhapta were *venari,* who had special circumstances, and ubir. This girl seemed to be in a group of her own, and he intended on finding out what that meant.

In the meantime, trying to keep her calm was like trying to bathe a cat.

"You can get whatever you need, but I'm coming with you," he said, turning off the ignition. Even with the still-mild September air, the breeze from the broken window would cool down fast, and they still had several hours to go. As they walked inside, he kept his eyes peeled for another car to boost. *Venari* tried to stay out of human civilization as much as possible, but he had needed to learn to drive a long time ago, and that meant learning to steal cars.

Kinza grabbed a basket and stalked down the aisles, throwing in seemingly random crap. Who needed a family-size bag of Doritos? She stood a solid foot shorter than him, and the bag looked as big as she was. Toiletries and snacks filled the basket. Never in his years as a *venari* had he purchased deodorant for an ubir. It's not like it was actually coming from his bank account, though.

Zaid took a deep breath and felt for the heartbeats in the store. Two of them were coming around the corner of the next aisle, and he heard keys jingling. As they rounded the corner, he angled his body to collide with a man with a receding hair-line and a horrid corduroy shirt.

As the man stumbled, Zaid moved his arm faster than human eyes could track and slid the keys from his belt loop.

"Whoops, sorry!" the guy said. Zaid just dipped his head in acknowledgment and pocketed the keys. He watched them move back to the pharmacy to wait in line.

Perfect.

When he looked back, Kinza was fiddling with something on a shelf but clearly eyeing the front door. As she turned back around, she jumped, seeing him staring at her. Honestly, she was the most conspicuous person he had ever met.

"Hurry up," he said.

She rolled her eyes, and the gesture made him want to strangle her. "How much do you get paid?" she asked.

"What?"

"How much do you get paid for capturing me? I'm dying to know."

"Fifty-thousand shillings."

"Pirate money?"

"What? No, Rhaptan shillings. It's equivalent to about two thousand American dollars."

"That's it?" she asked, wrinkling her nose. "I'm a little insulted."

He didn't know what to say to that, so just asked, "You've seriously never heard of Rhapta before? From your parents or relatives?"

"Nope," she said, heading up to the counter. "Not once." As the cashier rang up her stuff, Kinza looked at him expectantly. He pulled out a beaten-up credit card from his pocket. He'd get a new one every few years when the fake accounts started attracting the attention of the FBI. It came in handy when he needed to buy things outside of Rhapta, as the tribal city had a limited supply of modern niceties like sweat-wicking t-shirts and zip ties.

Kinza grabbed her stuff, and he followed close behind her out to the parking lot. "Not that one," he said as she walked toward the old beater. He clicked the fob on the keyring, and the lights of a silver pickup flashed a few spots away. She just looked at him with an unapproving stare.

As they got in, she asked, "So if these Abracadabra people have all these, like, powers or whatever, why hasn't it been in the news? I'm sure people would've freaked out by now."

"Anunnaki," he corrected. "And you are right. That's why it's hidden behind a barrier. Humans can't see it or cross it. I told you, all Anunnaki have to stay in the city."

"Or they get hunted down and murdered, yeah, yeah, I'm abundantly familiar with that part." She ripped open the giant bag of chips and started devouring them. "So let me get this straight," she said with a mouthful of orange dust. "A bunch of people with powers live in an invisible city in Tanzania, and they are not allowed to leave, right?"

"It's immensely more complicated than that," he said, pulling back onto the highway headed north.

"Sure, right, okay. I have a hard time believing that."

"And I have a hard time believing that you are not an ubir when you clearly have a tribal tattoo, *some* sort of abilities, and that *woman* had a Deathstone." Zaid was starting to get irritated. Maybe he should have put her in the trunk. "I think you're lying and that you are an ubir with some weird ability to hide your Aura and other abilities. I'm guessing you completed the rite recently, yeah?"

"That is *not* my problem," she said, crumpling the top of the chip bag and snatching a giant bottle of water. "I was living my life all by myself, and *you* ruined it. It's not my fault you and your stupid tribe got the wrong person. Maybe you should take it up with them before kidnapping and assaulting innocent people!" she yelled. "It sounds like you are all just a bunch of murderers that keep their own people locked up like animals."

Zaid's vision went red, and the buried image of his brother's body flashed in his mind. It took years of control not to shove her out the door and onto the highway. Instead, he yanked the steering wheel to the right causing the tires to screech and slammed the truck to a stop on the shoulder. Cars honked and swerved around them.

"Okay, you spoiled brat. You clearly know nothing. I'm getting that. But you should refrain from judging things you don't understand. If you're innocent, then great, the council will free you, you can go back to your special life, and I won't have to listen to your annoying voice a moment longer. Until then, have a shred of respect and keep *your mouth shut.*"

"*Excuse me?!*" Kinza dragged the words out, and he braced for a battle. "Who the hell do you think you are? I could not care less about you and your imaginary city. I wanted nothing to do with this. You followed me home. You blew up my house, not me, and do you think we can pay for that? No. Because the *hours* that I put into work go toward my tuition, and I'm not giving that up. And you physically injured my grandma and me. Pardon me, but you have not *earned* any respect!" She drew her feet up, crossed her arms, and turned her face toward the window, signaling the end of the conversation.

Zaid clenched his jaw, breath whistling in and out of flared nostrils. Without saying another word, he pulled back out into traffic.

THEY SAT in silence for two hours, the majority of which Kinza was fuming. The cityscape faded as they followed the highway up the side of Lake Michigan, the trees slowly becoming denser as they got farther north. For a portion of the drive, the sparkling water of the lake sat to their left before the highway moved deeper inland, and they were surrounded by trees on both sides.

As the hours wore on, she became curious again about Zaid's knowledge. Even though the story he was spinning was wild and totally unreal, he certainly did have a lot of details. Not once did he sound anything less than totally confident. In fact, he acted as if she should have *expected* this to happen. She wanted answers. Either way, she wasn't about to relinquish her pride; she still despised his entire being.

Quietly, she said, "Tell me more about the tattoos."

"Pretty sure it's my turn," he muttered back.

Swallowing her retort, she said, "Fine."

"Earlier, you said I followed you. Where exactly did you see me?"

"Yesterday, on the bus coming home from work. And when you followed me in the parking lot." She remembered the image of the dark-clothed figure and the way the light had shied away.

Zaid looked over at her. "I didn't get on any buses. And are you talking about when you ran into me?"

Kinza's brow furrowed, "No..." Her eyes went wide. "Wait. *That* was you? Then who was the other person? Another *venari*?"

Zaid looked as confused as she felt. "Describe them."

"Um, well, I couldn't see them at all, but they were wearing all black, like some sort of expensive ninja costume. And..."

"And what?"

"Well, it was like they were standing under a cloud, like even in broad daylight they would be in shadow. I don't know. It was weird and creepy. Friend of yours?" she asked sarcastically.

"I saw them as well, and I have no idea who they were, but they had a stable Aura, so they're Anunnaki for sure."

"An aura? Like meditation, third eye kind of stuff?"

"Yes and no. It's how Anunnaki tell each other apart. All of us have one. It's your... like your energy, your soul; an extension of you."

"Do I have an Aura then? Or do 'ubir' not have one?" She half expected him to give a detailed description of it, like it was a rainbow that glittered or something.

"That's the odd thing. You don't have one."

"What? No." She fake gasped, hand covering her mouth.

Zaid pursed his lips. "When Anunnaki complete the blood rite, their Aura shatters. That's how we, *venari*, can tell them apart from the rest of us. Besides the usual bloodthirsty tendencies."

"What's a blood rite?"

"It's my turn. Has anything else odd happened recently? Or ever? Like healing at an accelerated rate, visions, telepathy?"

"Telepathy?!" She almost laughed. This was getting so ridiculous.

"Yes."

"I've been having nightmares over the past week, but that's not like, supernatural though." She didn't dare tell him he looked like the warriors from her dream—no way, not a chance. "No telepathy," she added. Other than when she and Mitra occasionally locked eyes after a particularly bossy comment from Karin.

"Nightmares can have psychic properties, so I'm not ruling that out. Healing? Did you ever get sick as a child?"

"Yeah, I was sick all the time. The flu, chickenpox, even lice once."

"You said you've been having nightmares for a week? Well, what about now? Have you been healing since then?" he asked and nodded pointedly at her hands in her lap.

She turned them over and almost gasped aloud. The cuts from the rock were no more than faint pink lines crisscrossing her palms. It was as if it had been weeks instead of hours. She stared at them in disbelief. "Is... is that an Anunnaki thing then?" She almost didn't want him to answer.

"We all heal much faster than humans. See?" He turned his face toward her and pointed at his cheek. The gash she had given him was a faint line as well.

Kinza started to feel a little woozy. First, he knew about her tattoo, and now she had visible proof that both of them were healing much faster than anything she had ever seen. Not to mention that sometimes he moved so fast it was hard to track. He had said he could move at the speed of sound, right? Her heart started pounding a little too loud for comfort. She took several deep breaths, in her nose and out her mouth, trying to calm her frantic heart.

Trying to distract herself, Kinza asked, "So tell me again where we are going right now?"

"About another two hours north of here, there's a hotel where an Ummanu lives. He's a friend. He's got a portal we can use that will take us to a town close to Mount Kilimanjaro, and from there, we walk."

"What's an Ummanu?"

"They are..." He scratched at the scruff on his jawline. "They are humans who have agreed to keep the knowledge of the Anunnaki, but they live outside Rhapta. Kind of like assistants. No, that's not right. Haris would kill me for that comparison. Ah, well. Basically, they are all over the world, and they guard the portals for us, so we don't have to move too deeply in human society. They also help clean up any little messes we left behind. Like the commotion we left in your neighborhood last night. They'll pay off the local police to pretend it never happened."

"Mmm." This was not helping her frantic heartbeat.

Zaid looked at her out of the corner of his eye. She had forgotten he had mentioned something about "hearing" heart-beats. Great. "Are you well?" he asked.

It was an absurd question coming from the man who kidnapped her the night before and was taking her to a trial for a crime she didn't commit. She was fairly certain he did not give a modicum of thought to her wellbeing. "I need to pee."

He sighed. "Fine, we can make a quick stop. We need gas anyway."

TEN MINUTES LATER, they were pulling into a small gas station on the side of the highway. There were only two pumps, and the building looked like it had seen better days. Regardless, there were a few cars parked outside and one or two people milling around the door. The entire lot was backed by the thick forest that lined the highway.

Kinza knew that this far north, the woods would go on for miles, and the majority of houses were just cabins for people in the city to escape to on weekends and holidays. Gas stations like this were only around small towns for the locals to congregate, so there must have been a town not too far up the road. It would explain the number of people that were here.

She hopped out of the truck, it was getting close to sunset and the evening air felt good on her skin. She kept thinking about the healed cuts on her palms and realized that her headache was gone as well. In fact, she felt better than she had over the last week. She wouldn't say that the night prior had been any sort of beauty rest, but she hadn't had a nightmare, and that was a good sign. On the flip side, instead of feeling tired and lethargic, she almost felt *too* good. Her skin was warm, heart still pounding, and a restless energy thrummed in her arms and legs.

She wanted to call Grams and let her know she was okay and listen to her familiar voice. Kinza knew that Zaid wouldn't let her near a phone, though. As she motioned to go inside, he gave her a look that said *I'm watching you* and patted his calf. His obsidian blade must have been tucked into his boot. Kinza just curled her lip, wrinkled her nose at him, and walked inside.

The bell above the door chimed as she walked in. A pimply-nosed cashier looked up from behind the counter to the left and returned to his magazine when he saw her, blatantly bored with his job. She spotted the sign for the women's bathroom at the far back corner of the store and made a beeline for it. When she got inside, she locked the door and released a breath. It was the first time in twenty-four hours that she was truly alone. After using the toilet that might have been considered clean once in its life, she washed her hands in the sink and looked up into the cracked mirror.

As she had thought before, the dark circles were a bit better than yesterday, and her skin was a bit brighter. She was in severe need of a shower though, dust and grime from the past day's events coated her, even with a change of clothes. A few tiny curls had sprung up near her hairline, having been released from the sweat there. The faint remnants of tear tracks could still be seen on her face as well. She splashed some water on her face, dried her hands off, and left the bathroom.

She took her time meandering through the aisles of snacks, savoring her temporary freedom. She found a disposable cell phone, and as she turned it over in her hands, the bell chimed over the door as someone walked in. Immediately dropping the phone back onto the shelf, she peeked her head around the corner, expecting Zaid, but at that moment, she started to get that tingling sensation on the back of her neck. It wasn't Zaid.

The dark-clothed figure was walking right toward her.

Kinza's blood ran cold, and she dropped down, hoping they hadn't seen her. She quickly moved back to the end of the aisle to round the corner and looked again down the opposite aisle. The figure was nowhere in sight. Standing up, she craned her neck, looking around, trying to spot them, but couldn't see or hear anything other than the cashier ringing a few people up by the counter.

She moved quickly, walking to the front door, but the tingling on her neck became more insistent. As she was about to turn down the main aisle, the tingling became almost painful. Every primal instinct in her body suddenly screamed *down!* Kinza shoved her head toward her knees, and a long, deeply curved, obsidian blade whizzed over her head and embedded itself in the wall by the counter.

Chaos erupted.

The cashier started shouting as Kinza spun and lashed out with her arm in fear. It collided with the shoulder of the dark figure, and she stumbled backward to crash into a rack of trail mix and cheese puffs. The painful tingling had moved down and settled in her stomach, making the skin there burn.

The figure wrenched the sword from the wall, two people who had been at the counter ran out screaming, but the figure had no eyes for them. Kinza kept backing down the aisle, not knowing where to go. She looked left and right and realized the granola bars wouldn't help her.

They stalked toward Kinza, footsteps soft even on the sticky floors. They looked almost taller than they had the day before. Could this have been a different person? The hood was up but not as high as it had been the night before. She realized she could see their eyes. A green so faded it looked like all the life had been leeched out. A sickly color. They were narrowed in disgust, and the figure raised the curved blade behind them, holding one arm forward.

Kinza's back slammed into the glass fridge doors at the back of the gas station. She grasped for the handle and hauled the door open just as the blade came down, shattering the glass around her. She screamed and kicked out, miraculously catching her attacker in the gut. They bent over, and a distinctly male voice grunted in pain. She used the moment to turn and run the few feet to the bathroom, slamming the door shut behind her. She heard nothing at first but threw the deadbolt into the lock and looked around.

A loud booming came from the door, rattling it on its hinges and startling her. There they were. Kinza thought that it would immediately crack, but she realized the door was a bit thicker and heavier than normal. The bathrooms must have been the designated storm shelter for the building. Most public buildings in Michigan had to have them. He was trying to break it down. She guessed she had thirty seconds at best.

There were no other doors leading to the bathroom, and the only window was a small slit high above the mirror. She immediately climbed on top of the sink and unlocked it. It was tight and rusted, and one of her fingernails split down the middle as she pried it open.

A loud crack sounded through the door. It wouldn't hold long. She had to hurry.

She shoved the window open and stuck her arm out. She realized there was no way she could fit through it. The tingling on her neck and burning on her abdomen had become nearly unbearable.

"Somebody help me!" she screamed frantically, waving her arm. The window faced the back of the building to the woods. There would be no one there to help her. The door behind was truly cracking now. The booming was so loud it sounded like a thunderclap. "Someone heeeelp!"

When no one immediately came for her, Kinza jumped down. She only had a few seconds until the man would be through the door, and then she would be cornered. Without thinking, she punched the mirror, shards dropping into the sink. She didn't feel the pain as her knuckles started gushing blood. She just grabbed the largest shard she could and clutched it in her hand.

It was too late. The bathroom door flew inwards and slammed into the opposite wall. Kinza whipped around. The man moved like lightning, arcing his sword arm over his head in her direction. The world slowed, and Kinza felt herself screaming but couldn't hear it. Instead of the terrible pain of being slashed, the burning in her stomach reached a peak.

Suddenly, a bright, white light exploded out of her. A single wave of energy like a seismic clap followed closely behind. The man was thrown back through the open doorway to crash through the opposite wall. Kinza had a momentary feeling of déjà vu.

The walls and ceiling of the bathroom were destroyed, water bursting out of pipes, plaster falling from above. Kinza had dropped the glass shard, crouched down to avoid the falling debris, and looked around her. There was a hole in the back wall just big enough for her to fit through. She didn't wait, dashing to the hole, wiggling through it, and running straight into the waiting forest.

CHAPTER 6
TRANSIENT SALVATION

Zaid was just putting the gas cap back on when people started running out of the building.

He inwardly groaned but was immediately alert. He ran back to the driver's side of the truck and grabbed his second obsidian dagger, which was longer than the first he had just pulled out of his boot. Someone was shouting inside the building, and he could hear a commotion from the now open door.

What is going on?

He moved across the lot to the front door when a shadow dropped down in front of him from the roof. Zaid stepped back, his body moving on instinct, and barely missed the swipe of a roundhouse kick aimed at his head. The figure before him was draped in dark clothing, covering every surface of their body except for their eyes and hands. They got into a position he was intimately familiar with. Knees bent, one foot back, shoulders relaxed, and arms ready. It was the starting position for many Anunnaki fighting styles.

"Who are you?" Zaid asked. The figure responded by drawing a set of obsidian daggers similar to his own and slashed out, aiming for both his neck and abdomen. *Fine, be that way.* He twisted and parried with his own dagger, but one of their blades tore at his shirt, drawing the thin line of blood across his stomach. Hardly more than a scratch. He reached out with his Aura, searching for the other's mind. Only the solid wall of a mental fortress was available to him, but it was steady, unlike an ubir's would be.

Zaid ducked and spun as another swipe of the blade came one after the other in quick succession. He threw his left fist up, dagger in a backward grip, catching the attacker in the ribs. He rushed toward the figure again, but they launched up to grab around his waist, throwing them both back into a nearby car, its piercing alarm going off as metal crunched. He punched, ducked, rolled, and swirled away, getting behind them.

He had fought many ubir before and had years of training in Rhapta, but this was different. This was close. The shorter dagger had fallen from his hand, so he brought the other in a downward arc, but it was caught by a waiting fist.

Zaid twisted, but not fast enough. The attacker slashed at his neck, missing by several inches but still opening a huge gash across his upper chest. He grunted and slammed his head against the figure's own while he was still close, causing them to stumble back against the car and drop their other dagger.

Just then, he heard Kinza's scream come through the building.

That can't be good.

The attacker used his momentary distraction to lurch forward and grab Zaid's wrist with their bare hand.

Pain shot up his arm and through his body at the contact,

ruthless and unforgiving, bringing him down to one knee. He gasped as stars swirled in his vision, the pain in his body so complete he forgot his own name. He had heard of Anunnaki, who had abilities of pain, but experiencing it was something else.

It's unfortunate that you had to be here. You'll be nothing more than a casualty after this mission is complete. The voice came from inside his head, male and gloating. Zaid looked up and could see dark brown eyes crinkled in amusement. They were *enjoying* this. He could barely see through the pain that seized his muscles and clouded his vision.

The hand was instantly removed from his wrist as an explosion rocked the back of the building. Through the windows, he could see a body fly across the interior and debris falling in every direction. Shelves and racks of food crashed to the ground.

With the attacker's attention momentarily on the explosion, Zaid launched forward and impaled his dagger in the man's leg, and before he could retaliate, he shot up, sending his fist directly into the man's jaw.

The figure didn't even have time to scream and dropped like a sack of potatoes. Zaid sucked in a breath and yanked his dagger out, and reluctantly made sure he was still breathing. He only killed on the job when he absolutely needed to, and only ever ubir. Even years after the first time, he still felt vile and abhorrent the next day, needing to lock all emotion into a deep, dark place just so he could breathe.

Looking down, his own shirt was soaked in blood, the gash in his chest starting to pulse rhythmically. He checked for other serious injuries and, finding none, went inside.

The door chimed as he stumbled in. He reached out and could only sense a single heartbeat in the building. Picking his way through fallen shelves, he made it to the back, where he had seen the body fly through a wall. The pile of crushed drywall was there, water trickling from the ceiling, but it was empty. And the women's bathroom was obliterated, a gaping hole in the back leading right into the forest.

Dammit.

A faint sound had him whirling around. In the front doorway, a different figure was hunched, looking at him from over their shoulder. The same dark clothing wrapped around their body.

"Hey!" Zaid barked and was met by the same fortress of a mind. The figure dashed out the door, and he had to pick his way back across the fallen debris, wincing at the pain in his chest. By the time he burst outside, there was no one there other than the few people who had scrambled to their cars on the other side of the lot. A puddle of blood was on the asphalt near the car, but Zaid couldn't feel any other heartbeats.

They were gone. Something was going on, and he didn't like it. Never had he been attacked by another Anunnaki; only ever ubir. The first figure clearly had a pain ability, and the second he was unsure about, but they shouldn't have been so... *stable.* They had moved with precision and what was clearly years of training. Up close, their clothing looked distinctly Rhaptan as well, if an unusual style.

Police sirens came from a distance.

Zaid only knew one thing, someone was out here trying to sabotage his mission, and it looked more and more as if Kinza wasn't an ubir. Were they trying to kill him or her? His money was on her, but what was the purpose if Zaid was going to bring her in any way? What was she?

He had a sinking feeling the explosion did not come from the attackers.

Growling in frustration, he ran around the back of the

building. His vision swam a bit as the blood loss started to slow him down. Some wounds needed to be tended to; even with Anunnaki healing, they weren't immortal after all. He came out near the building's dumpster, which butted up against the dense forest, the shadows between the trees lengthening with the fading light of day. He reached out one more time, taking as deep a breath he could, and listened.

There. It was faint and growing fainter, but a heartbeat moved through the forest, away from him.

Kinza.

Years of training had him wanting to run after her so he wouldn't lose a mark. He desperately needed stitches, though, and even if he did catch up to her, he would probably pass out from the blood loss. He knew better than to attempt that.

He clenched his jaw, the muscle twitching, and headed back to the truck. The sirens were getting closer, and he wanted to avoid unnecessary human contact. It would be a royal mess if they found him here with no identity and no record of ever existing. No, he would drive to the nearest town, get the stitches, and then go after her. Ubir or not, he still intended on bringing her back to Rhapta.

The forest was deep, but he wasn't worried. He would catch up to her before morning.

Kinza stumbled through the forest, pushing away brambles and slapping cobwebs out of her face before they tangled in her hair. It was much darker under the cover of trees, and the air started to chill her skin. She kept looking behind her, expecting the dark figure to be on her heels, sword raised to strike, but after fifteen minutes of running, she started to slow down before she face-planted in the darkness.

The tingling on her neck had subsided, but the burning in her abdomen was fading slower. Pulling up her tank top to check for wounds, she gasped at the sight. The lines of her tattoo were glowing faintly, like embers in a fire. She poked and prodded at it, but it didn't cause any pain. After what had just happened, this shouldn't have surprised her as much as it did. She pulled her shirt back down, and thankfully it covered the glimmering lines.

She kept walking through the woods, hoping to find another road and hopefully a ride and cell service. Her mind was frazzled; jitters of anxiety made her hands shake. That had been the second time a room she had been in exploded. The figure's sword had been so close as fear had taken over, and the white light appeared again, pushing everything around her back. Now that she thought about it, when it happened the other night, she had still been in her nightmare, the vengeful hands of the warriors outstretched to grab her.

Zaid may not have been a hundred percent sane, but there was definitely something going on. There were too many things piling up that didn't make sense. Things that she couldn't explain. That was also the second time the dark figure had followed her, and this time they tried to kill her. Who would want her dead? She'd had normal parents, normal friends, never once healed quicker than she should have before today. Never once did light burst from her tattoo. There was nothing in her life that had been odd or supernatural.

Well... That might have been a small white lie she had been telling herself. A tiny little fib that kept the sheer panic of the last day's events at bay. She didn't want to think about her parents' mysterious deaths, or the unexplainable tattoo, or the freakish nightmares. So she locked those memories away for now and concentrated on trying to find shelter.

Within twenty minutes, the sun had set completely, and every sound of the forest at night made her flinch. A fear of darkness had never occurred to her until now. She had no idea where she was, and she was moving too far east, away from the highway. She didn't dare go back, though, for fear of the attacker or Zaid finding her again. In the back of her mind, a faint thread of regret wormed its way in, making her hope that Zaid hadn't been killed by the would-be assassin. It wasn't his fault he was a lunatic.

After another thirty minutes of walking, she no longer knew which way she was going. A few steps more, and a dim yellow light appeared between the trees. She peered at it and turned in that direction. As she drew closer, the edge of a large clearing came into view. It was someone's property; a large farmhouse sat to one side with a neatly tended garden of flowers, and an even larger barn sat on the other, and a large pickup truck and trailer sat outside. The light from the barn was what she had seen. It looked like it would be a quaint but beautiful home in the daytime. Every horror movie she had ever seen left her mind at the thought of a warm fire and a cup of tea. Maybe they would let her use their phone!

Walking up to the door, she was temporarily blinded when the automatic floodlights came on by the garage. The steps creaked as she walked up to the porch, and before she had a chance to knock, the inner door cracked open, and through the screen, Kinza could see an older man in his late sixties maybe, with a shock of gray hair on both sides of his head peering out.

"Who's there?" he shouted, his body angled behind the door. "I've got a gun!"

Well, that's not how this was supposed to go. "Sorry, sir, I uh..."

"Get off my property!" he shouted. Kinza heard whispering from inside the house.

"Wait, no!" she said, hands out. "I'm sorry to bother you so late. I'm lost. I—" She didn't think telling them that she had been kidnapped by a man with superpowers, only to be attacked by a ninja assassin, and then escaped when a light beamed out of a tattoo on her abdomen would get her anywhere. "The gas station up by the highway." She pointed back toward the way she came. "I was attacked by this crazy guy, and we all ran. I ran into the woods, and I was so scared I got lost. Please, could I just use your phone? I lost mine."

The man had one eyebrow raised in skepticism. There was an insistent whisper again from behind him. The man sighed and opened the door wider, "All right, my wife is adamant that you need to eat or something. Might as well come in."

"Oh my God, thankyousomuch!" She all but vomited out the words. She had been worried they would turn her away, and she would have to go back into the dark forest. She stepped inside a cozy hallway that led deeper into the house. White wainscoting covered the walls underneath old but well-kept floral wallpaper. A dark mahogany staircase went up the second floor.

"My name is Jack, and this is Josie," the man said, jerking a finger toward the woman behind him. Josie was several inches shorter than him, maybe a few years younger as well, but with a head of thick white hair styled in a bob.

Josie reached out and put a hand on her shoulder. "Oh sweetie, it sounds like you've had a horrible night! Were you with your friends or family at all? Was everyone all right? Wait," she said, ushering her down the hall and into a large kitchen lit by a lamp and a few candles. "Let's get you something to eat and a sweater or something. It's been getting cold in the evenings. Honey, will you grab the fluffy blanket on the wicker chair in the bedroom?"

As Jack went upstairs, Kinza said, "Thank you so much. Again, I'm so sorry to bother you. I've just had the *worst* night, I don't have my phone, and I need to call my grandma."

Josie gave her a sympathetic look, "Well, I'm not sure if you know where you are, but we are pretty far from the big town up the way, and there really isn't any cell service out here. But Jack will give you a lift in the morning if you're all right with that?"

Kinza hesitated but nodded. She didn't really have another choice.

"Okay," Josie said, patting Kinza's hand just as Jack walked in the room and handed her a giant blanket that was as soft as a lamb. She thanked him and wrapped herself up like a burrito. "Are you hungry? We just had some homemade chili for dinner, and I can easily heat some up for you. I make mine a bit spicy," Josie winked.

Kinza chuckled and said, "I love chili, thank you." She sat down at the island counter, and Jack sat at the stool on the end. "My name is Kinza, by the way."

"Nice to meet you, Kinza," Josie said as she moved about the kitchen, pulling out plates and mugs.

"So, go on, tell us what happened," Jack said. He was a bit rougher around the edges than Josie was, but it didn't bother her.

"I was up at the gas station by the highway, and I was inside using the bathroom when this man in a ninja costume came in with a sword—yeah, a real sword, and started swinging. It caused a huge mess knocking everything over, and he must have hit, like, electrical wires or pipes or something because part of the building exploded."

Josie and Jack had paused, frozen, staring at her with shocked expressions. "Well, shoot," the latter said.

"So that's when I ran out back into the woods and just kept running. By the time I slowed down, it was dark out, and I couldn't see anything until I saw the light on your barn."

"Are you from around here?" Jack asked.

"No, I'm from Chicago. My, uh, boyfriend and I were headed up north for the weekend." She inwardly cringed.

"It's Wednesday, though," Josie said, setting down a bowl of steaming chili and a mug of chamomile tea in front of her and one in front of Jack.

"Thank you, and, um, yeah. A five-day weekend, I suppose."

"Hmm," Jack said, sipping his tea. "I hope someone called the police and caught that ninja maniac."

"Me, too." She laughed awkwardly. Despite her need to lie, Kinza was relaxing, her shoulders felt less tight, and her heart had slowed for the first time in hours. It almost felt like being back in the kitchen with Grams and her lavender tea.

Josie leaned on the counter across from them. "Well, don't you worry, honey. We've got a guest bedroom upstairs and, like I said, Jack can give you a ride up to town tomorrow. They'll have better service there."

Jack nodded in silent agreement.

"Thank you so much," Kinza said. She and the couple spent the next hour chatting over random things. She told them about the college degree she was trying to get and her job, and they talked about all the renovations they had been making to the house over the years.

Josie had grown up just north of Chicago, and Jack was from up here. They told her about how they met when Josie had gone fishing with some friends and accidentally tipped their boat over. Jack, who was fishing closer to shore, dove in and pulled Josie to safety in a dramatic rescue. Only after they had gotten back to land did Josie tell him that she could swim just fine.

The three of them laughed hard enough for tears to form in Kinza's eyes and her stomach to cramp. It was all just so *normal*, she realized. No lost city, no supernatural beings, no one trying to kidnap or kill her, no white lights. Just a few laughs in good company and a good mug of tea.

When Kinza's eyes started to droop, Josie announced it was time for bed. As Jack locked up, Josie took her upstairs to a small bedroom at the end of the hall. It was just big enough for a bed, a dresser, and a nightstand. All the furniture was dated but in good condition. She brought her a spare set of pajamas that were a bit big on her but would work fine. After saying goodnight, Kinza closed the door and huddled under the heavy blankets. For the first time in over a week, she slept deeply and without nightmares.

Kinza woke in the middle of the night, needing to use the bathroom. She grudgingly climbed out of the warm bed and tiptoed down the hall to the guest bathroom. In her half-asleep state, she noted the excessively powder blue style, from the miniature bluebird figurines to the blue, clawfoot bathtub to the blue curtains. She smiled sleepily and came back to the bedroom a few minutes later. The house was old and creaked lightly with the wind. She almost found the lack of midnight police sirens and ambulances too quiet. The noise of the city had been a constant in her life, and this was probably the first time she had slept in a place so quiet, even with the creaky house. She was too tired for it to matter though, she eagerly shut the door, ready to crawl back into bed.

She had kept the bedroom window cracked just slightly, and the wind caused the lacy drapes to blow inward, letting the moonlight shine into the room. Fear, like a hot poker, speared her as the outline of a tall, male body stood before the window. She didn't get a chance to scream as the figure took two long strides and caught her, one hand going to her neck.

The last thing Kinza saw before she blacked out was a familiar bit of tattoo poking out of the man's shirt.

CHAPTER 7

ALLIES IN DARK PLACES

Kinza was slowly woken by the gentle rumbling of the truck and knew where she was.

She hated him.

She had been so close to going back home, back to her life, and here he was, ripping her back out again. There were those few, blissfully cozy hours the night before where she thought he wouldn't find her and she could go home. How had she been so stupid?

Opening her eyes, she sat up in the passenger seat... only to realize her arms were zip-tied to the door on one side and the center console on the other.

"Just a precaution. Seeing as you are prone to violent outbursts, I wanted to be sure you wouldn't make us crash," Zaid said it so coldly that for a moment, Kinza was reminded of Max and how he always wanted her to be silent.

"Are you joking?" she said, seething in her seat. She didn't even bother trying to break out of them.

"Clearly not," he replied, keeping his eyes on the road. "Can you blame me?"

She snorted. "Yes, yes I can. You also said you wouldn't knock me out like that again. So you're an asshole *and* a liar."

"Hey," he snapped, finally looking at her. "You also said you wouldn't run away, and yet I find you several miles away from the truck."

"Did you not see the man trying to kill me?!" she yelled. Taking a breath, she continued, "Also, where were you? I was screaming bloody murder, and I thought you wanted me alive?"

"I was attacked as well," he grumbled, clearly irritated at the thought. "There were two of them, and while I was trying not to die, you were blowing holes in the building."

The memory of the white light exploding out of her came back, and goosebumps ran down her skin. So she hadn't dreamed that. That was too much to think about right now, so she concentrated on the landscape passing. The sun was well over the treetops, and the clock on the dash said it was just past ten in the morning.

Zaid pulled the truck over and parked on the shoulder.

"What are you doing?" she asked.

He didn't respond, just took out one of his obsidian knives and cut the ties on her wrists. When he was done, he pulled back onto the highway.

"Thanks," she whispered, not really meaning it. "So, do you know who those people were?"

"No, but they are Anunnaki. Their Aura's were blocked off. I couldn't reach them, so I don't think they were ubir either. I have no idea what is going on." The last part, he said to himself more than to her. He had one hand on the wheel and head tilted back against the headrest. She thought he looked like he didn't want to be here almost as much as her. "We'll be there in thirty minutes and then another couple of hours once we get to Tanzania. Once we're in Rhapta, you can have your trial, and I can move on from this."

Great, sounds wonderful, Kinza thought to herself. They spent the rest of the drive in silence. As they got closer, they drove through more little towns and saw billboards advertising lakeside resorts, cozy cabins, and scenic byways. She thought about Jack and Josie and how they must have found her empty bed in the morning. The image of their worried faces made her feel guilty. She would have to repay them somehow one day.

Eventually, a little sign on the side of the road said they were entering Charlevoix, Michigan. It was a small town wedged between Lake Michigan and Lake Charlevoix, with a small inlet bisecting the town. It was clear the water was the appeal as tens of sailboats glided across the inlet, people jogged around boardwalks, and a lighthouse sat at the end of a strip that jutted into one of the lakes. She could see people walking along its length, even in the heavy breeze.

They crossed to the far side of town and drove a little further inland, and turned onto a boulevard that wound back into the heavy trees after another quarter-mile that came into a parking lot on what looked to be a historic inn. It was all white siding and white banisters with neatly painted black shutters on the multitude of windows. They got out of the car, and as they got closer, Kinza could see it was clearly a popular tourist destination. Through the windows, she could see throngs of people poking around in a gift shop and coming in and out of the lobby with pamphlets and gift bags. Zaid didn't go into the front door though, he walked to the end of the lot and started around the back of the building.

"Where are we going?" Kinza asked.

"My friend, Haris, is a groundskeeper here. He lives out back," was all he said and kept walking. She followed him to a small path at the back of the property that led back into the woods. It was well-kept, and at the end was a little cottage of red brick, a chimney to one side and a small shed to the other. Kinza thought that it was right up Grams' alley. As they got close, though, they could see the front door was hanging on its hinges. Zaid picked up his pace and jogged toward the door, pushing it inward. Kinza peeked over his shoulder.

The place was destroyed.

Tables turned upside down, dishes smashed on the ground, food smeared on the walls. The front door opened into a living and dining area, the fireplace to the left was filled with garbage. Curtains were ripped from the rods, and she could see picture frames broken on the floor down the hall to the right. Kinza had to tiptoe carefully into the room, just now realizing she was still in the pajamas Jack and Josie had given and had no shoes. *Thanks, Zaid,* she thought. He, on the other hand, strode through the rooms calling out, "Haris?" When no answer came, he shouted, "Haris!" a bit louder. There was no one home. He ran a hand down the back of his neck.

"Woah," Kinza said. "What happened? I take it your friend doesn't actually live like this?"

He just glared at her and said, "No, I don't know what happened. This must have been done last night, so they couldn't have gotten too far."

"And the portal thing?" She didn't see any mysterious-looking wormholes in the living room. Maybe he kept it in the bathroom.

"It won't operate without Haris's consent, and Ummanu are trained to defend Rhapta if need be. He wouldn't have taken anyone through. He would have either escaped or allowed himself to be taken. We just need to find him."

"Okay, but how?"

"My job is literally to track people down," he said with a

slight smirk; it didn't reach his eyes, though. "It won't take long. Let's just go." Kinza followed him out of the house, closing the door carefully behind them. As she turned to follow, she saw a carving in the doorway, a set of swirling lines, almost like overlapping infinity signs...

"C'mon!" Zaid barked from down the path. Kinza shut the door and jogged after him. As they walked back to the car, Zaid looked like a hawk, eyes focusing on everything around them, from the roof to the gravel to the people walking back and forth from the parking lot. He gave the area one last look before climbing into the truck.

"Do Anunnaki get attacked a lot, or is this just a 'me' thing?" Kinza asked when they got back on the main road.

"Ubir do cause problems sometimes when they are too far gone, but the real problem is when they move in packs. Sometimes two or three of them will group together and start to attack Ummanu. They are easy targets as they tend to stay in one spot with the portals. That, and ubir typically have a particular hatred for Anunnaki, and the best way to get revenge is to attack allies." He paused. "But, yes, getting attacked by unknown assassins is a 'you' thing."

"So, ubir attacked your friend then?"

"Most likely." He didn't say any more until they got to town. He pulled into a local supermarket and parked the truck.

"He's at the grocery store?" Kinza asked skeptically.

"Yeah, I think so," he said and got out of the truck. "Ubir do try to avoid busier public spaces. They are still sane enough to know humans will outnumber them if they are caught, so they never attack in places like this. Makes for a good hiding spot."

Kinza jumped out and stopped, remembering her bare feet. "I don't think they are going to let me in, though; maybe I should stay here?"

"Right, and have you run off again? I don't have time to be

chasing everyone around town today. And we don't know if those assassins are coming back or not." He looked around the parking lot and started peering into cars. After finding a satisfactory one, he broke the window and popped the door open. The alarm started screeching, and Kinza shoved her hands over her ears. A moment later, Zaid had ripped out a few wires under the steering wheel, and the alarm went off. He pulled a pair of bright pink Crocs out of the back seat and tossed them at her feet.

"Seriously?" she asked.

He didn't bother answering and just started walking toward the front door. Kinza huffed and shoved her feet into the too-small shoes. They must have been a child's pair based on the size. At least she wouldn't step on anything sharp, though. She followed Zaid into the store as he meandered throughout the aisles. It wasn't terribly busy at this time of day in the middle of the week. Kinza eyed the sandwiches in the deli.

"Can we..." she started, stomach growling.

"Later." Zaid strode to the back of the store, looking around again, eyes like a hawk. She honestly didn't know what kind of evidence he was hoping to find. A squished loaf of bread indicating his friend was there? But he went right to the back wall and pushed his way through the heavy flaps that said "Employees Only" that led to the stock rooms. Kinza just looked around, waiting to get caught. Thankfully no one was there as she and Zaid found another storage room further back. There was no window, but Zaid jiggled the handle. It was locked.

"Are you sure this is right? Why would he be in here? It's so *cold*," she said, shivering and rubbing her hands down her arms. It must have been a temperature-controlled area.

"Because I can hear a heartbeat inside," Zaid said and

pounded on the door with his fist. It didn't open, so he grabbed one of his knives and jabbed it into the handle, effectively ripping it off. He yanked the door open.

On the other side was a young man, about Zaid's age, with a shock of red hair and a family-sized can of tomatoes raised in defense. Upon seeing who it was, the man lowered the can, and a boyish grin tugged at his mouth. "Man, I have never been happier to see that beautiful face of yours," he teased.

Zaid just raised an eyebrow at him. "Glad to see you're still alive, Haris. Let's get out of here before we are thrown out. You can tell me about it in the car."

Haris moved to exit the storage room and caught sight of Kinza. The grin came back, and in the light, she could see a spattering of bright freckles across his nose that made him look younger than she guessed he was. "Well, what have we here? Are we working in pairs now? I thought there weren't enough of you for that?"

"I'm Kinza. Zaid kidnapped me because he thought I was an ubir, but maybe not, and now there are assassins after me. Nice to meet you," she said all in one breath. It was probably best to get all that out of the way before Zaid twisted the story in his favor.

Haris's eyebrow went to his hairline and gave Zaid a look. "Kidnapped, huh?" He grinned again. Kinza wondered if he was always in such a good mood and threw an arm around her shoulders. "Well, nice to meet you, Kinza. My name is Haris, and I would *love* to hear all about this kidnapping business."

"Let's go," Zaid said tersely and stalked out of the back, the two of them following closely behind.

"He's only like this because he cares," Haris whispered loudly enough for Zaid to hear. And to Kinza's skeptical look, he said, "It's true, he even smiled at me once," and winked.

Kinza couldn't help but laugh. She decided she liked Haris.

As they walked out of the supermarket and to the car, he kept his cheery smile, but she could tell both he and Zaid were eyeing everyone around them. When they got back to the truck, Kinza hopped in the front seat.

"Ubir?" Zaid asked immediately, looking at Haris in the rearview mirror.

Haris nodded grimly. "Three of them. One of them had some sort of compulsion ability extensive enough to keep me from moving my legs. Another had some sort of wind ability, blowing my stuff around, and the last was minor. She moved like a dancer or a gymnast or something. Super bendy. I heard them coming, they weren't trying to be quiet, and I almost made it out of my house, but the one had me compelled before I could blink. Thankfully, I had a Deathstone in my hand and dropped it, giving me enough time to get out."

"Deathstones? You mentioned those before," Kinza said, turning to Zaid. "What exactly are those?"

"In Rhapta, we have something called *magalkan'a*, or we usually just call it Aurastone," Zaid said. "It is a rock or a mineral, only found there and it amplifies our psychic connection, our abilities, our...everything. Some of our histories believe our abilities came from our proximity to the deposits in the earth."

"On the other hand," Haris said from the back seat, "*Reykalkan'o*, or Deathstone, is a piece of cracked Aurastone. When Aurastone is violated with either blood magic or removing it from Rhapta, it cracks and turns a cloudy color. It's physically painful for Anunnaki or ubir to be around."

"Like pounding headaches or ears ringing or something like that?" Kinza asked, thinking of the little stone Grams had taken out before she made her leave. She was starting to make a list in her head of things in her life that didn't quite add up, and she realized it was a larger list than she originally thought.

"Yes, exactly…" he said. His answer was not comforting to her. "So I take it you are not Anunnaki?" he asked.

"That's to be determined," Zaid said. "Right now, we need to get somewhere secure to rest."

"I've got another place nearby. I was going to head there anyway. I can give you directions."

"Can we *please* get me some food? I am starving."

"Zaid, are you starving your captives now? That's not like you," Haris mocked. "Even you need to eat outside of the city."

"Wait, what?" Kinza said as they pulled out of the parking lot. "You don't need to eat?!"

"*Venari* abilities are tampered down when we leave the city, and we can only be gone for a month at most at a time before we need to return to recharge," Zaid said. "But in the city, we can easily live off only one meal a day." He then said to Haris over his shoulder, "And I'm not starving her. She was the one who ran off yesterday, so I needed to knock her out for a bit."

Kinza just rolled her eyes. "So what now? Do you need to go kill the bad guys or whatever and *then* take me to Rhapta?"

Zaid sighed, and Kinza wondered if he had slept at all last night. "I don't know yet. We'll figure it out later. Now, will you please shut up so Haris can give me directions?"

Kinza gave him a death glare and mentally retracted her concern over her sleeping habits. She still sat silently in her seat, though, and looked out the window as they made their way across town.

TEN MINUTES LATER, Kinza was stepping into a small apartment that was nearly empty.

Haris had brought them to his "safe house," which was just an extra apartment he owned under a different name. It was two bedrooms with a balcony looking out onto Lake Michigan. The same beachy, white trim decor that seemed to permeate the town could be seen here as well. Everything was bright and airy, even if there was minimal furniture or personal items. Zaid immediately brought his duffel bag in and went down the hall to one of the bedrooms. A moment later, he came out and entered the bathroom, shutting the door firmly behind him.

"Not a chatty cathy today, I see," Kinza mumbled. "So the ubir won't find us here?" she asked Haris, who was digging around in the kitchen to the right.

"Most likely no," he said, pulling out boxes of cereal and a frozen pizza. "Not unless any of them have some sort of tracking abilities or training like Zaid. And I haven't seen anyone follow us. That being said, if you suddenly feel compelled to do something wildly out of the ordinary, speak up."

"That ubir, he can make people do things they don't want to?" she asked, sitting down at the kitchen table.

"Every ability is different, so it's hard to tell without them telling us outright. But true mind control is very rare. But either making people stand still or even forget the last few minutes is a bit more common. Small things like that."

"Oh, like Jedi mind tricks?"

"Yeah." He laughed. "A little like that. In most cases, it works much better on humans, and Ummanu, like myself, have a bit of training to be able to mentally fight it. It would be much more difficult on Anunnaki because of the psychic bond they all share."

"Ah, I see," she said.

Zaid came out of the bathroom in a cloud of steam. He had changed into a fresh set of black clothes, skin still damp from the shower. He dropped the duffel bag on the table and started digging around. "This is what is going to happen," he said sternly, eyeing Kinza. She crossed her arms and leaned back at his tone. "I'm going to leave to go track the ubir. You are going to stay here with Haris." He slid a few of the dark daggers into his boots and waistband. Kinza could smell the ocean scent of his soap. "If you leave," he said pointedly, "I will track you down just like last time, and the remainder of this journey will be enormously unpleasant for you. Is that understood?" He slung the duffel bag over his shoulder.

"You say that like any part of this has been pleasant," she sneered back.

"Trust me, sweetheart, it could get much worse."

"Sw—swee—" Kinza sputtered, ready to launch out of her chair. The anger was coming back in full force. It was like he couldn't go a few hours without purposely doing something to tick her off. Who was he to call her that? But she couldn't get a word in before he was striding out the door.

"I'll be back in a few hours," he said, and the door slammed shut behind him.

"So, ugh, pizza or raisin bran?" Haris asked cheerfully.

Kinza groaned and dropped her head into her arms on the table. "Pizza, please," she mumbled.

CHAPTER 8
UNTOLD SECRETS

Kinza and Haris ate mostly in silence.

She devoured half a pizza before taking a real breath. She could almost hear Grams admonishing her and telling her to chew her food for once. It had been almost two days since Zaid took her, and Mitra would also be worried as well. Kinza wondered if there were police reports out about her, maybe her face on a milk carton...

"I see you and Zaid don't get along much," Haris commented. He sat across from her, the remnants of his dishes before him. He had eaten the other half of the pizza and two bowls of dry cereal. Apparently, there wasn't much else for food here, but still, how could he eat so much? He was almost as tall as Zaid, but skinny as a rail. There was nowhere for the food to go.

"No kidding. Would you be friends with your kidnapper?" she asked.

"Hmm, I'm not sure. I've never been kidnapped, so it might depend on the circumstances. And I've always wondered if I would be susceptible to Stockholm Syndrome."

Was this guy crazy too? Apparently, the look on her face gave away her thoughts, because Haris barked a laugh. "I'm kidding, Kinz. I can see where you are coming from, though. Big, scary man appears and tells you you've been charged with a crime—" He paused and looked at her. "I am assuming he thought you were an ubir, am I right?"

"Yep."

"That's odd. As far as I know, *venari* have never been given the wrong target. What about the mark?" he asked, looking over her arms and neck. She stood up and lifted her shirt just high enough to see the delicate tattoo across her abdomen. Haris leaned back in his seat, looking stumped.

"I've had it for as long as I can remember." She let her shirt drop and sat back down.

"Do either of your parents have a similar mark?"

"No, I don't think they did. They died when I was young, so it's hard to remember."

"Ah, I'm sorry to hear that," he said gently. "I know what it's like to lose your parents. Well, my dad was never around, so I have no idea if he's alive or not, but my mom died of cancer a few years ago. It sucks."

"Was your mom Ummanu, too? Or how did you...."

"Oh yeah," he said with a slight smile. "My mom's family has been Ummanu for generations, and at least one kid always picks up the torch. I'm an only child, but I wasn't forced into it or anything. We are actually from Sacramento, and my mom, and grandma before she passed, both looked after a portal in the city there. Eventually, it shut down, but we found out a new one opened up here in Charlevoix, so we packed up our stuff. Just before we left, the cancer got really bad, and she passed. I still came, though. It's what she would have wanted."

"It sounds like you two had a great relationship," Kinza said, smiling. "You said the other portal closed? How exactly does that happen? To be perfectly honest, I'm pretty sure I'll still be skeptical about its existence until I see it... but I'm curious." She couldn't deny that Zaid wasn't entirely human, and she had seen the white light exploding out of her twice now; there was no forgetting that. But it was hard to imagine traveling through a portal to the other side of the world. And no less to go to a city and a tribe no one knows about. It was a bit of a stretch.

"I don't blame you," he said with a wry smile. "Like most Anunnaki history, it's hard to know for sure and even harder to study. What Zaid said before about the Aurastone and their abilities is true. It's only found within the city limits and nowhere else in the world. Some people, my mother's family included, believe that the portals exist outside of Rhapta, where there are deposits of Aurastone deep beneath the earth's crust, too deep to dig. And when the tectonic plates shift, and those deposits start to shift or crumble, that's when the portals open or close."

"So you don't open them yourselves?"

"Not exactly, we just guard them, but we have had ways to keep them hidden, and the knowledge on how to work them is passed down through generations." Kinza was starting to realize that Haris was a gold mine of information. She had learned more from him in the last hour than she had the entire time with Zaid. She looked at him eagerly, hoping he would go on.

"Ummanu history says that long ago, during the times of ancient civilizations, the city of Rhapta was accessible to everyone, Anunnaki and humans alike. Over time, humans became greedy or afraid, and it's not surprising as the Anunnaki would seem like gods to them. Wars broke out in the name of the Anunnaki. Humans tried to steal Aurastone, effectively creating Deathstone in the process, and the first ubir defected from the city. It was chaos. For those reasons, the Elders of Rhapta decided to bring the city into hiding, away from human civilization. The problem was ubir were already created, and most of them were too far gone to be saved.

"A smaller number of humans were still loyal to the Anunnaki and longed to help them, believing that if they could still help humanity through the ages. That was how Ummanu were born; a bond was formed between us. We agreed to watch over the portals, which only exist outside of Rhapta, and they agreed to let us keep the knowledge of their existence. Most of us are very proud of what we do, and while we never get to see Rhapta, we do get to interact with the occasional no-nonsense *venari* when they come through." Haris gave her a wink at that last part.

Kinza's eyes trained to the glass balcony doors across the room. She could see Lake Michigan from here. It was so large it looked like an ocean. People walked along the beach, kids flying kites in the still-warm September weather. The fact that there was a whole other race of beings moving around on Earth was hard to grasp. It was difficult to imagine a reality that you hadn't ever seen before, but it made the world seem so much bigger than she had ever thought it was.

How did these people fit into her future? She had imagined finishing her degree and starting some kind of urban development or maybe a social services career. Her whole goal had been to help people who could no longer help themselves, but did that include those who weren't entirely human? There hadn't been a ton of reasons so far that made her want to help Anunnaki, but she had only met one and had to believe that as a people, they were good. She wasn't really counting the ones coming after her as they sounded like an anomaly. That was also if they didn't charge her for being an ubir even though she clearly wasn't one. *I suppose they'll figure that out when I get there,* she thought to herself.

"You said that one of the histories was that the portals exist over Aurastone deposits deep in the earth. Are there other theories? I just don't understand how all of this stuff can exist and where it comes from," she asked.

"It is one theory, yes," Haris said. "Some people look to different avenues for explanation. For example, almost all of the portals exist around ancient monuments or sacred ground. There's one in Jerusalem, one near the Kashi Vishwanath Temple in India, Mecca, Easter Island... they are everywhere."

"I have a hard time believing that there is anything special about Charlevoix, Michigan," Kinza laughed.

"Ahh, now, don't be quick to judge," Haris said, waving a finger at her. "We are in the middle of the Great Lakes, and on what used to be Native American land and could easily still be sacred. About fourteen years ago, scientists even found something similar to Stonehenge at the bottom of Lake Michigan, with carvings of animals dated back at least ten thousand years. I'd say we are in a pretty special spot."

"All right, fair," Kinza said, putting her hands up. "So there are a lot of theories. Why don't the Anunnaki study the portals then?"

"Because they don't leave the city, they really can't. They are all connected by a psychic bond within the city limits. If they leave, they lose all of their abilities... healing included. They would start to lose their memory of Rhapta as well. But one Anunnaki long ago discovered there was a way to leave by practicing blood magic. I won't get into the gory details, but think blood sacrifices on a regular basis."

Kinza wrinkled her nose in disgust.

"Yeah, and the blood magic makes them start to lose their minds. They become more bloodthirsty and maniacal, and they are a danger to humans and Ummanu."

"So they created the *venari*, like Zaid, to track them down and bring them back." She thought she was starting to understand. Pieces were slowly falling together to form a larger picture. One of mythical beings and bloodshed.

"Precisely!" Haris seemed happy she was catching on.

"But how does Zaid get to keep his abilities and not go crazy?" She paused. "Wait, is that attitude of his an ubir thing?"

Haris laughed, throwing his head back. "No, no, that's just good ole' Zaid. There is a ritual the Elders perform on the *venari's* marks that allows them to go out into the world for a short time without losing their abilities. It's only temporary though, they need to keep coming back, or they will start to fade."

"Hmph," Kinza said, crossing her arms. "I think my theory was better. I don't know how you stand him."

"Zaid and I have been friends for years, and trust me. He's had some really bad things happen to him to make him the way he is. And his job is hard; he needs to act first and think later for a lot of it. If he didn't, he'd be dead several times over."

"I can't really think of any reason that would excuse someone from attacking an old lady and tying a girl up like a prize hog. And sometimes, he's just so *mean*. I mean, honestly, if he would have taken the time to explain why he needed to take me, I would have understood, and this whole thing could have gone much better."

"Really?" Haris asked skeptically. "You would've gone with the scary man speaking gibberish you didn't understand in the middle of the night?"

She felt a slight blush creep up her neck, "Okay, maybe not. But still, he could have been a bit nicer."

Haris exhaled a deep breath. "Don't..." He hesitated as if debating whether or not he should speak. "Don't tell him I told you this, but Zaid used to have an older brother. When he was thirteen, his brother disappeared without a trace. A year later, Zaid had finished the first portion of *venari* training and was going to be sent on his first mission. The Elders gave him his mark, and when Zaid tracked him down, he realized it was his brother. His brother had defected and became ubir. Zaid was forced to bring him in."

Kinza couldn't imagine finding out something so terrible about your own family. "That's horrible," she whispered.

"That wasn't even the worst part. When an ubir goes to trial, the Elders assess whether or not they can still come back or if they are too far gone, which was the case for his brother. So they made Zaid execute him."

"What?!" Kinza shouted. She shut out the thought of killing her own family, regardless of anything they had done. The thought made her want to vomit.

Haris grimaced and nodded. "*Venari* training is brutal, and punishment for ubir is even more so. The reason I tell you this is the next time Zaid is a bit testy, just remember it's not because of you, but every mark he goes after reminds him of the first."

Kinza thought about what would have happened if she had been in his shoes and found out one of her parents or Grams had been an ubir. The pizza was starting to churn in her stomach, so she took deep, slow breaths in her nose and out her mouth. It took three before her stomach settled again.

Haris caught on and said, "Hey, don't think about it. It was a really long time ago. Just don't say anything, okay?"

She nodded.

"All right," he said, standing up and putting the dishes in the sink. "Let's see what we can do about some clothes. But first, you smell like garbage. Please see yourself to the shower." He pointed toward the bathroom like she was being sent to her room.

Kinza smiled and said, "Yeah, yeah, I hear you." And then a bit quieter, "Thanks, Haris."

"No problem, kid."

She snorted. "Who are you calling kid? You can't be that much older than me."

He threw a wink over his shoulder and said, "Ah, but I am filled with much wisdom. To the bathing chamber with you!"

Kinza laughed. She had somehow gotten both more answers and questions than she had the day before.

Zaid fell into a familiar routine. Check with locals for unusual activity, listen for chaotic Auras, look for evidence of a blood sacrifice, rinse and repeat.

Before he had become *venari* he had thought the Elders giving out minimal information about their targets would make them immensely difficult to find. It turns out it's pretty easy to find a deranged lunatic hell-bent on keeping their abilities by performing human sacrifices. Especially when they ran in groups.

He sat in the truck at the back of the parking lot adjacent to a massive upscale resort thirty minutes southeast of Charlevoix. It hadn't taken him long to look through recent police reports in the area and noted a few missing people over in Boyne Falls over the last several months, and one body found completely drained of blood. As ubir spent more time away from Rhapta and completed more blood rites, they fell further into madness and cared less about hiding their kills.

He had never seen them stay at a five-star resort, though. That was new. Haris had mentioned that one of them had some sort of mind ability, so it was very possible they had compelled the staff to let them stay and to forget about them. It was actually pretty smart, hiding in plain sight. Zaid wondered if anyone else had been assigned to bring them in yet. He hadn't sensed any other Auras yet.

That was other than the violent, chaotic energy that was emanating out of one upper room. The resort was huge, three stories high, and at least three hundred and fifty rooms. It looked out onto a small lake, and the grounds were meticulously cared for. From his spot in the parking lot, he could feel the Aura coming from one of those rooms. It felt like someone was screaming inside his head while digging their grimy fingers into his memories. He blocked it off with practiced ease.

One of the first things he was taught in training was how to draw a line between his Aura and someone else's. A *venari* was useless if he couldn't at least keep hold of his own thoughts, and most ubir, especially those with mind abilities, would try to get in and tear him apart. Blocking off the ubir's Aura felt like a balmy mist coming down around the far edges of his mind. He relaxed a little for the first time today.

He had only slept a few hours the night before, which normally would be enough, but the stress of the last few days was running him ragged. It had only taken thirty minutes from the time he got back to the gas station in the early hours of the morning to finding Kinza at the old couple's house. Had she really thought he wouldn't find her? Climbing the drainpipe with ease, he had sat on the roof and waited for a chance to slip into the room. She had even left the window open. *Idiotic move.*

It had been too easy to step in and grab her the moment she got back from what he assumed was a trip to the bathroom.

When he had caught her the first time, he had felt no remorse, he was just doing his job, and she was any old ubir that he had to chase down. But something like guilt wormed its way into the pit of his stomach when he grabbed her the night before. Maybe it had to do with the fact this mission had been an absolute mess from the beginning. Maybe it was because he was starting to believe she wasn't an ubir and might be something else. Or maybe it was the gut feeling that he was leading her into danger that she sure as hell didn't deserve. There were too many unknowns, so it was hard to say.

He shoved those feelings way down and concentrated on the current job. This was clean and easy. He was *good* at this— no distracting emotions.

Zaid felt something push against his Aura from the right. He looked across the other side of the parking lot, and a figure loped along toward the front of the resort, sticking out among the gaggles of people in cable-knit sweaters and tennis skirts.

Bingo.

A man who looked to be in his thirties moved at a lurching pace, eyes roving around as if he was coming down from a drug-induced high. His clothes were dirty and wrinkled, and his hands clenched and unclenched as he walked. Zaid noticed as he went by a furious gust of wind drove leaves and debris across the lot, rattling against the truck for a moment before it faded. This must have been the one with the wind abilities Haris had mentioned. Elemental abilities weren't uncommon, but their level of usefulness depended on the user's power and control. This one looked pretty average, despite the damage done to Haris's place.

As the man walked in the front door, only a few guests turned to look at him, but the valet didn't even acknowledge his existence. The mind one definitely compelled the staff not to notice them. This was going to be tricky with all the people around.

He put the truck in reverse and pulled out of the lot, already forming a plan in mind.

CHAPTER 9
PLEAS NOT UNHEARD

Zaid attempted to keep up with his mother as she wound her way through the crowd. He could hardly see over the throngs of people, but he knew his mother could. That was her ability; she had the eyesight of a hawk, able to see hundreds of yards away with a crystalline clarity.

He just focused on the bright teal of her dress, trying not to lose his way. It had been almost a year since he had been tapped to be *venari*. If he had been picked on before, he was all but ostracized now. Some people recognized the changes in his tattoo as he walked through yet another plaza and shied away from him. Bounty hunters were known to be both dangerous and unlucky, apparently even before they started training.

When Savar had marked him nearly a year ago, he had told Zaid's mother he would have one more year before training. She had protested, saying he wouldn't be done with his schooling yet, but Savar had insisted on their desperate need for more *venari* and Zaid's ability. That had been solidified a month later when they found out about his second ability; to hear heartbeats. It was like he was created specifically to hunt and catch his prey.

His mother had told him it would be all right, and she would try to fix it, but Zaid knew better. He slowly stopped looking longingly at every warrior that walked by, knowing he would never be one of them. No, he was doomed to the dark pit that was bounty hunting, and time was running out.

They passed through another plaza near the center of Rhapta and came to a massive structure. Before him was one of the many temples that sat at intervals around the city, and they were always teeming with life. The structure was shaped similar to the Pyramids of Egypt, except it appeared to have steps on the outside leading to the top, which held a huge, azure Aurastone. Not as big as the one in the central plaza, but still large. The inside of the pyramid was hollow, though and the ground level was almost entirely open to allow people in and out. It had limestone floors set with a myriad of mosaics and a skylight in the ceiling to allow visitors to see the Aurastone from within.

Zaid's mother walked quickly through one of the entrances, with him following closely behind. With the one-year mark coming up quickly, his mother had formed a vague plan to keep him another year.

But she wanted to pray first.

The fact that she needed the help of a deity did not seem like a good sign to Zaid, but he said nothing. Anunnaki had many names for the deity they worshipped, but it was always the same being. The giver of the Aurastone. Without Aurastone, many believed the Anunnaki would not exist, that it was a gift given to them to mine and worship. And in return, they would stay in the city and pray, giving glory back to the deity that bestowed it upon them.

People knelt in the center of the temple, looking up as they prayed. They prayed for continued good health, for their children to manifest great abilities, for the Elders to never die, for even longer lives, and for the ubir to disappear. It was one of the few places in the city that Anunnaki let their Aura show visibly. During most times, the psychic Aura that connected everyone within the city limits was invisible, but Zaid knew that everyone had their own Aura representative of their soul.

As people prayed, they each let theirs shine. There were deep indigos, and cyan, and bright orange ones. He saw Auras that glowed copper and some pulsed a dull red. One woman in the corner had one of a soft, dove gray and the man next to hers was an almost imperceptible yellow. No one looked up as they entered, each within their own mind.

Zaid's mother knelt within the circle of people, motioning for Zaid to do the same. She looked up, took a deep breath, and closed her eyes. As she let her breath out, her Aura came to life. Hers was lavender, similar to the tiny four-petaled flowers that grew on vines in the western quarter. They always grew around cracks in the stone, spreading in abundance as nature took over. The flowers reminded him of his mother at times when he would hide in that area of the city, reminding him to come home.

He took a deep breath and closed his eyes as she did, then he let it out slowly. Zaid didn't need to open his eyes to know what his Aura looked like. He had seen it many times and typically kept it hidden as it didn't help others' attitudes toward him. It was always midnight black and as beautiful as the night sky. His mother would say that she could see tiny stars twinkling within it, but he never saw any. He was pretty sure she had made that up.

As he knelt there with his eyes closed, he thought about what to pray for. He figured he should pray for a way out of this *venari* business. But again, he knew better than to ask for that. He thought about praying for health or wealth or power, things Amir would ask for, but that didn't feel right either. In the end, he just asked to simply be good at his job, and then maybe someone would look at him like he mattered. Someone other than his mother, of course.

When he was done, he peeked over and saw his mother was still in prayer. He closed his eyes again and let his senses fan out, listening to the overlapping rhythms of the many heartbeats in the chamber. The deep beat was soothing, and knowing so many people knelt around the same circle, all for the same purpose, made him smile. No one fought, or bickered, or shied away from him. They all just closed their eyes and prayed.

Zaid looked around the central plaza that was filled with people. On the east and west sides of the plaza sat long, rectangular pools of water. Children splashed in the pools while parents and the elderly sat on the lip. The north side of the plaza began one-half of the long boulevard that bisected the city and at its entrance was a huge statue of a king long forgotten. In the center was a cart-sized Aurastone that pulsed faintly. People passed by to place their hands on its warm surface. It was the largest ever excavated. And on the south side of the plaza was the Grand Hall.

The Grand Hall was one of the largest structures in the city. It was symmetrically shaped in a plus sign with the northern wing extending into the plaza. That wing of the building was wide open and supported by enormous limestone pillars. The other wings of the Hall housed the Elders, who never left, as well as various council rooms and various administrations.

One of those rooms was their destination now.

Zaid followed at his mother's heels as she climbed the wide, sweeping steps and entered the open building. Once inside, his skin started to cool in the shade. Members of various councils walked around in color-coded robes, and citizens came through on various errands of business. As they walked deeper into the building, Zaid saw a few old men in white robes. Each of them wore a large necklace of obsidian beads with the bottommost bead being made of Aurastone.

Elders.

There were fifty of them on the Chief Council, and none of them were under the age of seventy. That wasn't as young as one would think because Anunnaki lived slightly longer than humans, but it was still old. Every major decision that came out of their chamber dictated what the future of Rhapta would look like. One out of every fifty was named Grand Elder. The Grand Elder was always someone with a prophetic or psychic ability. They would speak the future of the Anunnaki race in an attempt to guide them in truth and wisdom. The current Grand Elder Hakim was older than the sun, blind as a bat, and generally spoke in riddles. The only reason he was still allowed his position was that his visions were never wrong. It wasn't unusual for Anunnaki to have a vision once or twice in their lifetime. Especially with the amount of psychic energy that enveloped the city. But Hakim spoke of things that would come hundreds of years in the future. The average person might see that it might rain the next day.

Long ago, Rhapta used to be a monarchy. Who the first was is a topic of discussion, but a single bloodline ruled the city for thousands of years. The most prominent history says that a few hundred years ago, the last king of Rhapta died in his bed. His most trusted vizier went to inform the crown prince, but he was nowhere to be found. They searched for years, never to find the last heir to the ancient Rhaptan throne. In desperate need of a government and wanting to avoid a power vacuum, the remaining viziers formed what is now the current council of Elders.

It was one of these Elders that his mother was going to see. Elder Ishar. He represented the *venari* and was known for being strict and taciturn. Ishar followed the rules of the council above all else, and his mother was going to remind him of those rules. Hopefully, he wouldn't take it negatively.

They came to the west wing that housed many offices for the Elders' personal use. In one such office, they found a guard standing just outside the open doorway and Ishar sitting at a desk within. Zaid's mother stepped up to the door only for the guard to block her path, obsidian-tipped spear in hand.

She cleared her throat, and Ishar looked up from his papers with shrewd eyes. *Let her in.*

His mother entered the chamber and stopped before the desk. She bowed her head in respect, and Zaid did the same. His mother had told him to keep quiet, and he had no plans of doing anything else.

Thank you, your grace. My name is— she started, but Ishar cut her off.

I know who you are, Ekaja Hatem. And I know why you are here. He looked over to Zaid, his obsidian necklace swinging with the movement. *You want to plead for the boy, am I right? You would like him to have some other apprenticeship. Well, I'm afraid I cannot help you there, it has already been decided.*

Thank you for the consideration, your grace. But I merely came to remind you of the rules your council set in place for this city.

Ishar's bushy white eyebrows rose, but he said nothing.

Your very council decreed that all children must *attend school until their fifteenth year. Zaid is only in his twelfth. I ask that you keep that rule enforced and allow him to finish his education for the remaining three years.*

Ishar gave her a long look. Zaid knew Ishar's abilities as all children did. He could see everyone's Aura all the time, whether they showed it or not. He could be found looking at the edges of a person, deciphering their Aura before responding. The exact time was also always known to him, but he was the only one who found that interesting.

I'm sorry, Ms. Hatem. The need for venari overshadows the need for the boy's schooling. It had already been decided. He looked back to his papers, clearly dismissing her.

Zaid's mother wasn't one to back down easily, though. She stepped forward. *Please, your grace. I beg of you, give him more time.*

Ishar looked up, irritated now. *I have already—*

Oh, come now, Ishar. She only wants what is best for her child. Another voice spoke as cool as a tundra winter behind them. Zaid turned to find Elder Tahir standing in the doorway. He was one of the youngest members of the Elder Council at the age of seventy-seven but looked no older than fifty. Cold black eyes looked at Zaid with mischief and winked.

Tahir, the rules are—

Yes, yes, the rules are there for a reason. But was that original reason to make sure children have a certain level of maturity before starting on their internships? We wouldn't want our poor boy Zaid here to miss out on some valuable lessons over the next few years. Especially when they could be crucial to his apprenticeship.

Ishar sighed. *We cannot wait another three years, there are just too many ubir.*

A year then, Tahir said. *Let's give the boy another year with his mother and his classmates before he starts his training. And then, if need be, we can provide him with a tutor to continue his lessons during the apprenticeship.* He placed a hand on the boy's shoulder.

By the look on his face, Zaid knew Ishar had lost this argument. He gave a single nod. *One more year.*

Zaid's mother beamed and thanked him profusely as they followed Tahir out of the chamber. When they had walked a bit down the hall, she turned to him. *I cannot thank you enough for your input, your grace. I have already lost my husband. I cannot lose one of my precious sons so soon.*

Not to worry, Ms. Hatem. And I think our boy Zaid here will excel at his career. They both looked back at Zaid, and Tahir gave him a warm smile. Zaid decided he liked the Elder. *Now I'm off to a council meeting, but enjoy your year, understand?*

Zaid nodded vigorously, and they watched the Elder walk away. White robes swishing and tendrils of ice trailing behind him on the marble floor.

As Zaid and his mother descended the wide staircase of the Grand Hall into the plaza, he caught sight of a familiar slight figure.

Amir! Zaid called out. The young man, now sixteen, turned at the sound of his name and smiled when he saw them. Bounding up the steps to them, Zaid could see the faint blue whorls at his bare shoulders, the marks of a scholar. He also saw his tattoo on his left side, looking so *normal,* and he had a slight pang of jealousy.

That all went away as soon as Amir's hand fell onto his shoulder and the familiar calm descended around him. *Hello little brother. What are we doing in the central plaza today?*

Amir lived in the scholars' building just two plazas away now and only came home once every few weeks to check in. Zaid missed him, but knew it was what made him happy.

Hello, my darling son, their mother said, kissing him on both cheeks. *We have just petitioned Elder Ishar for another year for your brother before he starts his training. We were almost denied, but Elder Tahir stepped in, and our request was granted.* Zaid wanted to point out that his mother had petitioned nothing and had been faintly chastising the Elder, but didn't say anything.

That's wonderful! Amir said, hugging him about the shoulders. *Another year of schooling will be good for you. But you said Elder Tahir stepped in? Be careful of him. Hunar says he is dangerous and more clever than anyone realizes. I would make sure he doesn't try to get you to do something in return,* he warned.

Amir! Don't say such things. And you shouldn't be listening to every word Hunar says, you know he involves himself with unsavory people. Hunar was Amir's mentor, and many people knew he didn't adhere to any status quo within the city. While Rhapta remained mainly peaceful, the outskirts and slums were another matter. They existed outside the psychic barrier and therefore had weakened access to their abilities and their Aura eventually faded. It was for people who either didn't want to live within the city's strict rules or couldn't afford to. Funding for the outskirts was scarce, and people grew sick and went hungry more frequently than within. There was even talk of many rebel groups forming who wanted to oppose the Elders and the Rhaptan way of life, stating that they should be able to leave the city whenever they wanted.

The outskirts of the city were still within the psionic shield that hid Rhapta from the rest of the world, but as soon as one left, they would solely become human. Except for ubir. Gossip around the city mentioned various names of scholars, merchants, and even warriors who fraternized with the rebel groups, but it was never proven. Hunar was one of these.

Mother, he is my mentor and a very smart man. Smarter than many people realize. Did you know that he once proposed a theory that there was actually a way for us to leave the city and go out into the human world without losing our abilities? How wonderful would that be!

Ack! their mother said. *I don't want to hear this talk from you. Stay away from people like that, please? I just want you safe.*

Amir looked less than pleased but said he would and bid them goodbye. The entire walk home, Zaid thought about the human world. He knew bits and pieces of it, just what they were taught in school, but to walk its cities and talk with its people? Amir was right; that would truly be a wonder.

CHAPTER 10
SHATTERED RULES

Kinza wiggled her fingers in the strips of sunlight coming in through the blinds, watching as it created patterns over her skin.

She was lying in bed in the other bedroom in Haris's apartment. Thankfully he had given her a spare set of clothes that fit her surprisingly well. The shower had done wonders at wiping away the grime and dirt and fear of the last few days. It was a miracle what a little soap and water could do for a rattled mind. Grams would probably tell her that water had some special properties of healing or something like that. Afterward, she had passed out on the bed only to be woken up an hour later by Zaid's deep voice rumbling in the kitchen.

She could vaguely hear them talking about the ubir. Zaid must have found them, which wasn't surprising. She closed her eyes again, hoping to fall back asleep, but it wouldn't come. She was too wired with thoughts of portals and ancient species and blood sacrifices.

A fist pounded on the door. "Come out here. I know you're awake."

Zaid.

Kinza sighed and ripped the blankets off. If he could leave her alone for once, that would be just peachy. She padded out into the kitchen, where Haris was eating a can of beans straight from the pot. "Did you find them?" she asked Zaid, who was leaning against the counter.

"Yes, we're leaving as soon as this garbage disposal finishes his fifth meal of the day," he said, nodding to Haris.

"Excuse me, some of us have a high metabolism and need to eat," Haris said, shoving another spoonful in.

"So, where are they? What exactly are we going to do?" Kinza didn't know how she was supposed to take down a fiendish Anunnaki who could bring down tornadoes, but she was fairly certain she had a good swing if she could get her hands on a crowbar.

"*You* are not doing anything," Zaid said. "You and Haris are only coming with me, so I know where you are, and if things go sideways, I don't have to race all the way back here to protect you."

"See," Haris said to Kinza, waggling his eyebrows, "I told you he cares. He's just a big softie." He reached out as if to hug Zaid, but the man turned into a blur and was on the other side of the room in half a breath. Haris just laughed as Zaid brushed a non-existent piece of lint off his shirt.

"I'll leave a few weapons in the truck just in case," Zaid continued without acknowledging Haris. "But I'm hoping it shouldn't take too long. They won't know I'm coming, and they wouldn't expect either of you to show up anyway."

"Are we actually going to take them back with us?" Kinza asked. The thought of a rabid man in the backseat the whole way to Tanzania sounded less than thrilling.

"Not unless any of them look like recent defectors, I'll just have to kill them, and yes," Zaid said, noting Haris's expression, "I do have the right to make that call. I can't bring four people in, and I can't let them roam free." He turned to look at Kinza, "I need you to promise that you will not leave the truck. I can't have you getting in the way and screwing everything up. Yes?"

Kinza scowled at him. Of course, he thought *she* was the one who was going to be a problem, and not the ubir. "Yes, you're highness," she grumbled. His attitude was becoming really insulting, childhood trauma or not.

"Perfect, meet me out in the truck in ten."

"THEY'RE LIVING *HERE*?!" Kinza asked incredulously.

She was looking out of the window of the truck at a huge resort. It looked like the kind of place that parents who paid thousands of dollars for their kids' preschool would go on a weekend getaway. Her parents had taken her to Wisconsin Dells once when she was really little, and they had stayed in a moldy-smelling motel. Her mom had taken all the little soaps, and Kinza felt fancy using the factory imprinted bars in the bathroom back home. They laughed and played in the waterparks the entire time there were there, and Kinza didn't have a single bad memory of the trip. It was her first and only vacation experience.

Kinza had expected the ubir to be camping in the woods or hiding behind a dumpster, but not here. What were they doing? A facial in the morning only to sacrifice the masseuse in the afternoon? Now was probably not the time to start giggling, but she couldn't help it.

Zaid glared at her in the rearview mirror and shut off the engine. "Something funny?"

"I really didn't expect us to be tracking down a bunch of ubir at the Hoity Toity Hotel. Are you sure Haris and I can't get a massage while you do what you need to do?" She giggled again, and Haris huffed a laugh, clearly trying to keep it down. It just made Kinza laugh louder.

Zaid just rolled his eyes. "Just stay in the truck, both of you. I'll be back in thirty minutes."

"Okay, make sure to grab the fancy soaps, will you?" Kinza barely managed to get out, Haris couldn't hold back his laugh this time, but Zaid only shut the door on them.

The hotel was packed. It was almost like being back in the central square in Rhapta with the amount of heartbeats Zaid heard around him, but there was way more vocal noise.

He had gone through the main entrance and slipped through the halls unnoticed. There were too many people around for any of them to notice he didn't quite fit in with the crowd. Mentally orienting himself, and walked down the carpeted halls toward the rear of the building that faced the lake. He let the barrier of his own Aura down just slightly, only enough to be able to sense the others. The waves of malicious energy were coming from a few different places. One was moving through the building a floor above him, and there was another on the other side of the building. But where was the third? Haris had said there were three of them.

Zaid took the stairs, foregoing the packed elevators to the second floor. The building was shaped in a large rectangle, and he was on the side closest to the parking lot, where he had felt the cluster of Auras earlier in the day. He headed further in that direction.

He spent a good deal of his life wandering around human cities, and generally, his missions took him to the darker places; back alleys, abandoned parking lots, or deep in a rainforest. Rarely did he need to actually go into society. He had the money and fake credit cards, but he was trained to avoid interacting with the humans unless he really needed to. Walking through the honeysuckle-scented halls and passing smiling families was not something he was used to. His only interaction with "people" was back home, and he hadn't had more than a few days off in years.

Zaid froze, feeling an Aura moving parallel to him further down the building. The hall he was in bisected the building and ended in another hallway running perpendicular. He hesitated before turning though, he could feel the other Aura further down the hall to his right. As they got closer, he could feel the pulsing rage emanating out. Each Aura, ubir, or Anunnaki felt different and looked different too when they were visible. He imagined this was a slimy, dishwater color that felt acidic when you got too close. The feeling almost made him physically recoil, but he stood still, listening for footsteps.

When the steps slowed down the hall, he peeked around the corner. Another man looking a bit younger than the first. He looked a bit cleaner and his movements less erratic, but the Aura was unmistakable. Sometimes he wondered who these people had been, if they had family back in Rhapta or if they were all alone. The Anunnaki population was large and the city larger, so the chances of having met this man or his family were slim, but still. He thought about it.

The man pulled out a keycard and entered a room, second from the last. So that's where they were camping out.

Zaid waited a few minutes to see if anyone would come

back out. He only felt one Aura and had planned on picking them off one by one anyway. A couple came out of a room down the opposite end of the hall. Zaid leaned against the wall nonchalantly and gave them a polite smile as they walked by, each one had beaming white teeth. When they were out of sight, he crept forward.

He had hardly taken a step when another Aura appeared in full force right behind him. Whirling around, he barely had time to throw a fist when a slender body slithered around him with unnatural grace. She, clearly a woman, climbed onto his back and wrapped her thin legs around his neck, effectively cutting off his air supply. He tried to gasp, but her grip was so secure the edges of his vision started going dark almost immediately.

Zaid reached for his dagger just as everything went black.

Kinza bounced her leg on the center console. She was sitting in the back seat, looking out toward the front doors. It had been almost forty-five minutes, and Zaid still wasn't back.

"I think something is wrong," she said, nibbling at a fingernail. It's not like she actually cared. Honestly, if he was killed, she would be free to go home to Grams. Problem solved. But in the back of her mind, she knew that even if Zaid died, they would just send another *venari* after her.

"Just relax, he's fine. He literally does this all the time. He's probably just trying to do it in a way the guests don't notice."

"Mhmm."

Haris turned around in his seat to look at her. "For real, I've been friends with him for a few years now and have helped him on a few missions once. 'Helping' generally involved me playing 'getaway driver,' but he's very good at what he does. I've met other *venari* who are much older than him, and he makes them look sloppy."

A family with a gaggle of kids was headed down past a line of trees to the beach, where tons of other people lounged. It was already a bit too cold to swim, but the sun looked warm on the sand, and kids carried buckets and shovels. Another five minutes went by, and Zaid still wasn't back.

Kinza sat up and grabbed Zaid's duffle bag off the floor, and unzipped it.

"What are you doing?" Haris had spun around again.

There were more daggers and long knives than she had expected. Some of them were all obsidian, and others were made of bone and others of bronze. There was a long coil of silvery-gray rope. She reached out to touch it...

"I wouldn't—" Haris started. Too late. Kinza sucked in a breath as she felt a faint zap. She snatched her fingers back. "Interesting."

Kinza looked at him with wide eyes, "What exactly about that is interesting? And what is that?"

"It's *laqueus*. Basically, rope that has properties to subdue Anunnaki and ubir abilities. It's only mildly annoying to them, but to humans or Anunnaki children, it's physically painful to touch."

Kinza avoided touching the *laqueus* and dug out a small bone knife, just small enough that she could stuff into her back pocket. She left the larger daggers in the bag and grabbed a black zip-up hoodie that was lying at the bottom. It came down halfway to her knees when she put it on, but the hood was deep enough to conceal her hair and most of her face. On the off chance that the two assassins followed them, she didn't want them to find her so easily. Maybe they wouldn't recognize her.

"No," Haris said. "Absolutely no. Put those back and sit down."

"I'm just going to go and take a look. I won't get in the way. I'll stay by other people, so I don't stand out—"

"You look like a hooligan! Just stay in the truck."

"I'll be right back. You watch the truck," she said and hopped out.

"You are going to get yourself killed, and I'm not exaggerating, Kinza please—" The sound of Haris's voice was cut off as she closed the door. She only got a few sidelong glances as she walked to the front of the hotel and entered the lobby. White marble floors gleamed with gold accents, and fresh flowers sat on every possible pedestal. To the left was a copse of plush sofas arranged around a fireplace, and on the left, a baby grand piano sat in the light of the windows. The double doors were kept wide open to let in the afternoon breeze. Kinza stood in the doorway, taking it all in.

"Staff enter through the side doors."

Kinza turned to find an older doorman in uniform looking at her. "I'm sorry, what was that?" she asked.

"Staff," he punctuated, "enter through the northside doors." He looked her up and down as he said it, nose wrinkling at her clothes.

She had half a mind to shout at him that she would never stay in a place that treated people like garbage, but making a scene would be the opposite of "not getting in the way." "Ah, okay, thanks," she said instead and went back out. There was a manicured path leading from the right of the front doors along the north side of the building. It took her quite a while to walk to the other end, but eventually, she found a secondary parking lot that she assumed was for the staff. There was also a smaller, unmarked door that she assumed was her designated entrance.

A group of what looked like waitstaff was entering through the door, and the last woman was struggling to carry an overly large silver tray covered in the remnants of food. They must have been coming up from the beach or one of the large gazebos she had seen farther out down the property.

Kinza ran up to the woman. "Here, let me help you," she said and lifted the other end of the tray.

"Oh honey, you have impeccable timing. I was about to drop it. Thank you!" She looked to be in her fifties with carefully coiffed graying hair and expressive blue eyes.

"No problem. I know how it is," Kinza replied, trying to fit in. They wiggled through the doorway, Kinza strategically letting the woman go first so she could lead the way. The walk was longer than expected to the kitchens, but she shouldn't have been surprised by the sheer size of the building.

"Do you work in the kitchen?" the woman asked. Kinza saw that she had a gold name tag pinned to her uniform that read "Meredith." All the staff had variations of beige or dark green attire and were neatly presented. Not a hair out of place. Kinza wondered how she thought she was going to go unnoticed going in the staff doors; Haris was right; she did look like a hooligan compared to everyone else.

"Ah, no. I clean rooms, just didn't get a chance to change yet." It wasn't entirely untrue; it was just a simpler version of the truth.

They had made it to the massive kitchens, which looked to be at least three long rooms and set the tray on a side counter. People in white aprons ran back and forth, a red-faced man in a chef's hat barking orders at the souls unfortunate enough to work under him. Wait staff bustled in and out of the room in clusters taking steaming platters of food. Everything from ornamental pineapple towers to crème brule to a whole turkey could be found lying on silver platters shined to perfection. In stark contrast to the beautiful food, most of the kitchen staff looked like they were on the verge of tears or a mental breakdown. Kinza's dad used to watch war documentaries late at night, and the re-enactments weren't nearly as terrifying and chaotic as the hotel's kitchen.

"I would hurry on up, hon. Marcus is in a hell of a tizzy today and fired two people before the lunch bell. Can you believe that? Before the lunch bell. By the way, I'm Meredith," she said, sticking out her hand. She had no idea who Marcus was but assumed he was in charge here. She made a mental note to avoid people with that name on their nametag.

Kinza smiled and took it. "Kinza, nice to meet you too."

"Well, I gotta hurry," she said, eyeing Kinza's clothes. "And I'll pray for you. You'll need it if Marcus sees you."

Kinza chuckled. "Thanks, see you around." She hoped Meredith did pray for her, but not because of Marcus. She watched her run out of the kitchen and deeper into the building.

Looking around, Kinza realized she really did need to move, but going back out into the hallway seemed like a good way to run into the wrong waitstaff. She snuck her way through the kitchen, trying to avoid platters of food or tripping on dropped leftovers. She had made it to the other end of the room without getting spotted and entered into the next room of the kitchens. This one seemed to be slightly colder with metal racks lining the sides and filled with an assortment of fresh fruits, vegetables, chilled cakes, and spare ingredients. There were slightly less people in here, so it was easier to move along the aisles.

A breeze moved through the room, ruffling towels and aprons and causing Kinza to shiver. Why would there be a breeze? There weren't any windows in this part of the building. As she got closer to the end of the room, the faint tingling sensation crept across her neck and down her spine. The feel was starting to become familiar, and she kept her eyes and ears open when it didn't fade away. A moment later, movement caught her eye in the adjacent hall running along the kitchens. Kinza quickly ran over to the doorway and looked around the corner.

Amid the swarming staff was a man lurching through the halls, almost as if he was drunk. The staff moved around him like a river around a rock, seemingly unaware of his presence. The breeze had gentled but still carried the faint scent of unwashed body from his direction. She almost gagged in disgust. If she could imagine what an ubir would look like, this would be it.

The man turned down another hall, Kinza moved to follow, staying as quiet as she could. He kept going down the hall, still in the staffing area of the building, passing storage rooms and offices. He was maybe thirty feet in front of her when someone stepped into her line of vision.

"What is this?" a voice snapped. It was a short man with mousy brown hair and thin lips. Kinza's eyes snapped down to the nametag.

Marcus. *Crap*. "Uhh…"

"In what world did you think it was all right to come to your place of employment dressed like *this*?! You are given a uniform for a reason and are expected to be ready and dressed fifteen minutes prior to your shift and to never show up in your… streetwear," he said in disgust.

Kinza saw from over his shoulder, the ubir had stopped in the middle of the hallway and turned to look in their direction. Unfocused eyes looked directly at her, and she had a sudden overwhelming sense of panic. She couldn't grasp any of her thoughts, as if they were caught up in a whirlwind and wouldn't come down.

"Now you are going to need to come with me..." Marcus was saying. But Kinza wasn't paying attention as the ubir started running down the hall toward her.

This was not good.

CHAPTER II
SHACKLED MIND

The tingling at her neck was at an all-time high, running down her spine to spark the heat in her abdomen. The familiar feeling only increased the panic in her mind.

No, not here! Kinza thought to herself. The ubir had started running toward her, there was a minuscule chance that he desperately wanted to talk to Marcus, but she wasn't willing to bet her life on it.

"I'm going to have to ask you to hand in your nametag and uniform, Miss—" Marcus started.

"I'm so sorry about this!" she shouted and stuck out her leg, causing one of the waitstaff walking by them to trip right into Marcus, both of them landing in a heap and causing a blockage in the hallway. "Sorry!" she shouted again and turned and ran.

The ubir would have to stop and pick his way around the jumble of people, giving Kinza precious seconds to run through the halls and attempt to locate Zaid. The task was daunting as she passed door after door, looking for a way to the main part of the hotel.

A thumping behind her had her turning to look. She wished she hadn't as the ubir was lurching after her at full speed, his long legs eating up ground faster than she could run. Thankfully he was unsteady and kept crashing into the walls and shoving people out of the way. Kinza was much more nimble and dodged around vacationers as they shouted at her and the ubir.

She had to find Zaid. And fast. He had mentioned the ubir were staying in one of the upper rooms, but she had no idea which one. Her best chance was to run in that direction and hopefully into Zaid. A sudden gust of wind hit her back hard enough for her to stumble, but she kept her balance. It knocked over a vase of flowers, the ceramic shattering on the floor. More people were noticing.

A stolen glance had her heart beating faster in her chest; the ubir was only a few feet behind her. She dodged a group of people and grabbed onto a doorway, propelling herself into what looked like a ballroom. At the moment, it was filled with people joined together, a violinist in the corner and an instructor counting the steps. People screamed as Kinza and the ubir shot through the room, the latter knocking people to the ground. Her lungs were starting to burn.

As she entered the next room, she was jerked back by the hood of the sweatshirt, and she slammed to the ground coughing. The ubir growled words she didn't quite catch and shoved her back down as she tried to sit up. Kinza tried to shove him off, but he was too heavy. The metallic scent of dried blood filled her nostrils. He shifted and put a knee on her stomach, and wrapped his hands around her throat. He grinned as he mumbled, "You filthy little..." she didn't catch the rest.

The heat grew in her stomach at the same rate as the panic.

She clawed at his hands around her throat and gasped for breath. People were shouting in the other room, and she tried to quell the growing heat. If the white light exploded again, people would die. She was sure of that. There had to be another way out. There *had* to.

She stopped clawing at his hands, allowing the weight to come down completely. It forced her eyes closed and tears to leak out, but it let her reach into her back pocket. She grabbed the handle of the bone knife and plunged it into the ubir's thigh. He screamed and jumped away.

Sweet, sweet air flooded her lungs as his hands let go. She scrambled to her feet as the ubir howled along with the wind flurrying throughout the ballroom. Decor fell to the floor, and the glass rattled in the windowpanes, but only for a few moments before dying down. Maybe he couldn't sustain it longer than a few moments at a time?

Still coughing, Kinza ran from the room past a hotel security guard who was just running in. She pointed behind her to the ubir struggling to his feet, growling obscenities. Not pausing to watch, she fled.

Zaid groaned and lifted his head. The inside of his skull was throbbing, but upon wiggling his fingers and toes, everything seemed attached and whole. The problem was he was tied to a chair.

"Are we awake, princess?" an oily voice asked.

A man came into focus across the room. He was in one of the hotel rooms, he realized. There were two queen-sized beds to one side of the room, a desk and two tall dressers to the right, and Zaid in a chair in the middle. Based on the light in the room, there must have been two tall windows behind him as well. The man, the ubir he had seen walk into the room, sat on the edge of one of the beds, looking at him with a smarmy smile and eyes slightly out of focus. Up close, he had light brown skin and thinning hair. It looked like his nose had been broken a few times as well.

"I wondered when they would send one of you," the ubir mused. "I had thought you would come sooner, but I should just be happy with the freedom I've had so far, right? No matter," he said, standing. "I don't plan on going back."

"Freedom?" Zaid croaked out. His throat was raw, so his swallowed twice, trying to work some moisture back in. "You have no freedom. You're bound to your own madness."

The ubir circled Zaid's chair only to stop right in front of him and bent over, hands on his knees to inspect Zaid's face. "And yet you're the one who needs to run home every turn of the moon like a whipped dog, begging for scraps. I've always wondered, do they make you fight for the chance to go back out, like a prize or something?"

"You really like to hear yourself talk," Zaid said, chuckling.

It's better than listening to your inner ramblings, his voice said from inside his mind. The closeness of the voice made him feel like his mind was violated, coated in a foul-smelling substance. He wanted to scrub his mind clean. The ubir must have heard the thought because a wide grin split across his face. Zaid mentally shoved him out and allowed the cool, balmy mist to surround the edges of his mind.

The ubir frowned disapprovingly and stepped back. "Where are the others?" Zaid asked. "I know there are three of you."

"Ah yes, I'm sure your little Ummanu friend told you all about us. He was a very good sport about our visit. So accommodating, but I wished he had stayed around. I wanted to play with his little portal." He turned a mocking frown in Zaid's direction. When Anunnaki left the city to become ubir, some walked straight out and into Tanzania and found their way from there. Most aren't very good at navigating the human world, though, and end up staying in the eastern portion of Africa. But some plan ahead and make it out further through planes or just on foot.

Most Anunnaki never took the portals unless they were *venari*, or the occasional Elder if need be. So the chances of an ubir knowing how to operate one was very low unless by some off chance a *venari* becomes ubir; that's always bad. Everyone knows that the quickest way back to the city is by portal, though.

Many of them, and he assumed Slimy here was included, develop crazy plans to attack the city if they are far gone enough. They say that they are freeing Rhaptan citizens from the Elder's iron-strong clutches. It was the madness talking, really. The only thing that would happen if they got to the cities borders is they would be taken down immediately. Guards patrolled the city, and Elder's monitored the psychic bond; there was no way an ubir would make it two feet into Rhapta.

The ubir hummed. "Well, let's see, Basma is hanging from the rafters in one of the ballrooms. You met her earlier." He winked. "And Ghassan…" He tilted his head as if he was listening. After a moment, he raised his eyebrows and grinned. "It seems Ghassan is playing a fun little game with your partner through the halls. Causing quite a ruckus, I would say." His eyes flickered, focused and unfocused as if he were here and not here.

"My partner? Bounty hunters don't work in pairs, or is your mind too addled to remember that?"

"Hmm, Ghassan is chasing a little bird quite intently, and

the only people Ghassan truly wants for the blood rites are Anunnaki, so they must be with you."

Anunnaki... *You have got to be kidding me.* Zaid mentally groaned and cursed every god in every religion he knew. Why? Why did he have to get her? Why couldn't the Elders have given this assignment to someone else? He could have been finished with this one days ago.

It was time to change the plan. "Yeah, my bad, forgot to mention that little change. I would suggest you untie me before she gets here, too. You see, she's got this wonderful little ability to take away any Anunnaki's abilities. She's probably toying with your companion down there before she renders him completely human."

He saw the ubir's eyes widen just a fraction, but he said without inflection. "You're lying. Tell me the truth." The last part he said with compulsion. On anyone else, it might have worked, forcing him to spit the truth out whether or not he wanted to tell it, but not *venari.* It was an attestation to how far this ubir's madness had gone that he had forgotten all *venari* are trained to lie. If, on the off chance, they are taken by humans and need to pass a lie detector test, they can. Not that it would prevent the FBI from locking him up for a lack of a verifiable identity, but it was a useful skill.

Zaid steadied his breathing, slowed his heart rate, let his eyes dilate, and lied. "My partner has the ability to take away Anunnaki abilities."

The ubir swore, now pacing the room. They were always lured into the life by the promise of freedom. Freedom to live as full Anunnaki, but outside of the city. The thought of becoming human was generally abhorrent to them. Zaid watched as he moved around, muttering to himself. He took the distraction to slip one of his wrists free; they honestly weren't tied all that well. It was an unskilled knot of hunters who didn't expect their prey to escape.

Zaid didn't believe for a second that his daggers were still on him. He assumed they had all been taken. When the ubir made another pass across the room, Zaid took a chance and shot an arm out toward him, grabbing the front of his shirt and slamming his forehead into the ubir's. He yelped and jerked back, and Zaid went with him, chair and all to fly forward in a heap. Half the chair cracked and split apart, and all but his other arm was free. He used it to smash the remaining pieces of the chair on top of the ubir, and it shattered around them.

Zaid stumbled back a step, but it was a second too long because the ubir screamed and barreled into him. He was heftier than one would imagine, and it took some effort to haul him off, but not before he got in a good crack to the jaw that had him seeing stars.

Blinking around them, he got to his feet just as another fist came flying in his direction. He deftly maneuvered around it and kicked a leg out, sending the ubir to the ground again. Zaid grabbed his foot and hauled him closer. As the man tried to sit up, Zaid threw another punch, sending his head cracking back down.

Just as he was about to start pummeling him, something speared into his mind like an anchor. He only had half a breath to realize it was not good when the voice was inside his head, uttering commands.

STOP. Zaid stopped. The ubir was breathing heavily and got to his feet. *DON'T MOVE.* He punched Zaid in the eye, and Zaid did nothing. He couldn't; the compulsion was deep in his mind like a fish that swallowed the hook.

The ubir got to his feet and gave him a joyless smile.

KNEEL. Zaid knelt. He kicked Zaid in the stomach, and

again he couldn't react. He tried to pull the anchor in his mind out, but it was buried too deep.

TURN YOUR HEAD TO THE RIGHT. Zaid turned his head. A now-bloody fist came swinging again, this time landing squarely in his nose. Blood gushed out, and the pain had his eyes watering. He could do nothing as the ubir gave him command after command, each followed by another kick, punch, or elbow. His left eye started to swell shut, blood dripped into his mouth, and he couldn't spit it out. The last kick was aimed at his ribcage, and it was hard. He felt bone fracture as the air whooshed out of him.

Zaid kept kneeling before the ubir, trying to pull the anchor out of his mind. He was facing the window as the ubir stood before him, the light coming in giving him the most ironic of halos. Another oily smile was plastered on his face. He looked like he was enjoying this.

STOP BREATHING.

Kinza was pretty sure her legs went numb minutes ago. The hotel was huge, and she had zig-zagged almost its entire length dodging families and staff members. Apparently, the hotel's security hadn't fully grasped what was going on.

She wasn't dumb enough to think she had stopped the ubir, so she didn't slow down. And sure enough, she heard screams again, and a strong wind hit her back. Thumping foot-steps came after her, slightly out of sync. He was limping.

Good.

She avoided the elevators and aimed for the utility stair-case at the end of the hall, praying that it wasn't locked. Slamming into the door at full speed, it opened. The relief was short-lived as she turned as she saw the ubir coming down the hall after her like a rabid dog. She let the door slam shut and knocked over the garbage can in the stairwell, hoping it would slow him.

The twisting flights of stairs looked ominous as she started to climb. When she got to the second floor, she heard the door slam open below. The ubir cursed as he tripped and fell over the garbage can and howled in pain. He must have landed on his leg. She kept climbing, though, air coming in gasps. She was honestly surprised she hadn't passed out yet, she wasn't much of a runner and hadn't seen the inside of a gym since high school, so the fact that she was still going was impressive.

The third-floor stairwell came into view, and she yanked it open and started running in the opposite direction, back down the length of the hotel. She only got a few steps when one of the room doors opened, and a young man started to step out. Without thinking, she shoved him back in and closed the door.

"Hey!" he shouted as he stumbled back into the room. He had salmon pink shorts and a hideous sweater on. It must have been some current fashion trend. "Who are—"

"Shh!" she cut him off. "Please just shut up a moment." She held her breath and put her ear to the door. Sure enough, she could hear the stairwell door slam open and thumping foot-steps pound down the hall. Her heart pounded at twice the speed as the footsteps came close and then passed the door headed down the hall.

"Excuse me; this is not your room. Are you high or some-thing?" the guy asked, grabbing her shoulder. She shoved him off harder than she meant to, and he stumbled again and fell to the floor.

"Sorry about that," she whispered. "Have a nice day." She cracked the door open and peered out to the right. She saw the retreating form of the ubir and a few guests jumping out of his way. Quietly, she went out into the hall and closed the door softly. Walking slowly back the other way toward the stairwell, the tingling sensation prickled on her neck, and she took a cautious glance over her shoulder. She was steps from the stairwell door, but down the length of the hall, she could see the ubir running toward her again.

Oh no...

She shoved back into the stairwell and saw it went up another half a flight. *Roof access.* The sign said alarms would sound, but she pushed through to the roof and heard nothing but her own labored breathing and the thumping footsteps getting closer.

The top of the roof was completely flat, with only a short wall running all the way around. Large ventilators and an army of air compressors were scattered around, and Kinza ran between them, ducking down.

The roof access door swung open, and she heard the ubir step out and stop. Kinza tried to slow her noisy breathing and moved behind another compressor, keeping low.

"You are here... I know this," the ubir said in a jumble of words. His voice was like sticky molasses. She could hear him move across the roof, trying to find her. She kept moving further away from the sound of him, hoping to find another door. But too soon did the edge of the roof come, and she could see the lake from where she stood. Looking down, it was too high to jump. She would surely break the majority of her bones, if not her neck.

"Nowhere to run, birdie?" Kinza whirled around, and the ubir emerged from between two large ventilators. Madness danced in his eyes. Looking at someone who truly couldn't be reasoned with was like having a violent animal in front of you. You either had to run or attack. And she had nowhere to run.

Kinza patted her pockets.

"Looking for this?" he held up the bone knife, still covered in blood. Looking down at his leg, she could see the tear in his pants, but nothing other than a faint scar remained. He looked at her greedily, and Kinza's skin crawled.

She backed up, the wall hitting the back of her thighs. Nowhere to go.

"Tell me, birdie, can you fly?" Wind erupted around them, tossing leaves across the roof and into Kinza's eyes, her hair blowing wildly into her face. The ubir ran right at her with the bone knife as she tried to see. The moment she could, he was there, and she twisted and pulled his arm toward her.

He went right over the edge of the roof.

CHAPTER 12

BONDS BETRAYED

Zaid walked down the brightly lit streets, pulling his hood up to fight the glare of the neon signs and kept his target in view.

He had been following the man, or ubir really, for almost half a mile through downtown Osaka. Hundreds of people walked in streams around him, but he kept his eye on the hooded man a few meters up. He had been given his first assignment, and while both nervous and excited, it was proving to be much easier than expected.

When Savar had given him the location of the first ubir, he spent hours trying to do research on the country of Japan, its people, culture, and language. While Anunnaki mastered languages much faster than humans, the thousands of characters boggled his mind. He also had no idea how he was going to find one person in millions.

He had arrived that morning, traveling through the portal just outside of town. The Ummanu there, an elderly man, greeted him and gave him directions to the city. It had taken a few attempts to understand the train system, but he arrived eventually. The level of sound was what unnerved him the most. He had spent quite a bit of time in the outskirts of Rhapta the last few years to get used to verbal speech, but it was still new to him.

When he arrived in the city, he spent hours wandering around wondering how he would find one ubir in this city. He had paused at a bus stop and reached out with his Aura searching that way. What he found had him physically recoiling. The violent, chaotic energy that was an ubir's Aura hit him like a bus. He had felt an ubir's Aura in training a few times as they were being brought in, but they had always been bound. This one was a good half-mile away, and it felt like it was sizzling his skin.

It hadn't taken long from there to find the lurching figure meandering through the crowds in a near-aimless direction. Zaid continued to follow him, slowly getting closer. He wanted to wait until they were in a less populated area before jumping him, but it seemed as if that would never happen.

At some point, the ubir turned down a small side street at the edge of downtown. Zaid pushed his own Aura down and followed him by heartbeat from there. The further he walked, the less people there were. Only a few couples walked hand in hand, sharing bags of pink and blue fluff and meat on a stick. Human clothing and food were still odd to him despite his training, but it was interesting.

The ubir was about to turn another corner when he half-turned back. He must have caught sight of Zaid because he took off running.

Zaid groaned and followed. He ran but not too fast; he didn't want to catch the attention of the humans or their government. They ran through alleys and side streets, past shops advertising skincare and little cartoon figures in bright flashing lights. It was hard to concentrate on the figure, so he let the Aura guide him. Zaid stayed just a few feet behind him, waiting for the right moment when the ubir suddenly turned into a ramen shop.

The line of people winding out the door shouted at them, thinking they were cutting, but Zaid followed the ubir through the restaurant and into that back kitchen. He had to stop him now before someone got hurt. This was getting too close.

As the ubir ran through the kitchen, Zaid put on the slightest burst of speed and grabbed his hoodie. The ubir twisted and fell to the ground, and Zaid hovered over him.

Got you, he said, smiling and ripped the hood back.

Zaid's vision narrowed to a pinprick as the maniacal eyes of his older brother looked up at him. The eyes, so familiar and not at the same time, focused and unfocused. A wild, disturbed grin split his lips upon seeing Zaid's face. *Hello, little brother.*

Zaid fled the restaurant.

He wandered the streets for a long time. Long enough for the sun to set completely and the heavy nightlife to pop up. Fliers were waved in his face, people snapped flashing pictures of each other, and music screeched at every corner.

He heard and saw none of it.

The fervent face of his brother on the last night he had seen him over a year ago was the only thing in his mind.

Zaid had enjoyed his last year in school, despite the looks he received. Over time, word spread that he had been tapped, and the way he and his mother were treated declined drastically. He spent as much time as he could climbing the baobab trees and stealing *guakal* from the vendors, and talking with his best friend Khalil as much as he could.

Amir came home less and less, spending more time with his mentor, Hunar, and a ring of other scholars. Every time he came home, he was more excitable and talked louder about the things the scholars knew. Their knowledge apparently went deep into the history of Aurastone, Rhaptan kings, and prophecies.

Amir would spend his meals at home talking about the things the Elders kept hidden from them, citing that they were in control of the ubir, or that they were keeping us all locked up, or that they killed the last Rhaptan king. The wild talk had his mother shouting at him, and they always ended in a screaming match. Zaid would run outside just to feel the sweet night air until they stopped.

Eventually, Amir would come out and apologize, placing the familiar weight of his hand on Zaid's shoulder, and a gentle calm would move through him. A few times, he begged Amir to just act normal when he came home, but his brother always said he needed to do what was best for their family. This would help them somehow.

Just after Zaid's thirteenth birthday, Amir had come home one night out of the blue. He burst through the door, stumbling around flipping through papers and going into his old room to search through a chest. He hadn't been home for months before that, after he and Mother had a particularly nasty fight.

Amir! What is this? What is going on? She stood and followed him into the other room, Zaid trailing behind. Amir whirled around to look at her, and he saw his brother's eyes were frantic and slightly dilated.

Where is it?! Where is the red book with the gold letters? I need something inside it! he said and resumed his search.

My son, are you drunk? Or have you taken some sort of weed? What are you talking about?

Amir spun around again and looked at them both. He lurched over to their mother and grabbed her shoulders. *It's Tahir! He knows, but he doesn't know that we know! I have to... I have to go.* He went back into the main room.

Amir? Zaid asked. The skittish look in his eyes frightened him. He had never been so worked up before.

His brother turned to look at him and grabbed his arms. *Don't trust him, Zaid. Do you understand? He doesn't know that we know, and I only have so much time... I have to... I have to confront him... I need to know the truth...*

That's enough of this! Mother shouted. *I will hear no more of you talking slander of the Elders.*

Amir didn't even seem to hear her, he just turned and left. He never even found what he was looking for. That was the last time Zaid had seen his brother. A few weeks later, an old scholar and a few guards came to the house and asked about Amir's whereabouts. He had been missing from his apprenticeship.

Zaid's mother started to panic and went from house to house asking around for Amir. Apparently, another young scholar and one guard had gone missing as well. Things like this were never a good sign. It usually meant they defected and either went out into the world and slowly became human, or completed a blood rite and became an ubir.

His mother refused to believe either, but Zaid knew better. She always wanted to believe the best in people, but he had gotten good at seeing things for what they were. Amir had been hanging around people connected to a rebel group over the past year, and he talked in frantic bursts about deep, hidden knowledge and glorified living in the human world while still being Anunnaki.

Zaid and his mother went to the temples many times, and every time he asked that his brother would be okay, but it felt like his request was falling on deaf ears. Over time the chances of seeing his brother again grew slimmer and slimmer. His mother cried for days and smiled less as if Amir had taken a portion of her Aura with her. And when it was time for him to go to training she begged the guards not to take him. He told her it would be okay, though, and would come to see her when he could.

Seeing his brother today brought back that initial panic, though. While he knew that Amir becoming an ubir was a very real possibility, he couldn't reconcile the idea that his older brother would choose to sacrifice another person; that he would use blood magic. Amir had always wanted to leave the city, but enough to kill someone? The idea refused to take root in his mind.

Zaid continued walking down the street until he could see a small park up ahead over the heads of the crowds. He had a growth spurt recently and had shot up several inches. He already towered over his mother, and she said he probably wasn't done growing either.

The little park with a nice reprieve of green grass and a small koi pond in the middle. A white gazebo sat to one side and fairy lights hung in the trees. It wasn't like Rhaptan nature at all, but the break from the harsh lights and booming music of downtown was a relief. It wasn't anything like the calming weight of his brother's hand, but he wasn't one to want things he couldn't have.

The bench on the gazebo creaked as he sat down. Orange and black koi fish swam in zig-zag patterns through the water, completely oblivious to the things going on in the world and the choices he had to make. What was he supposed to do now?

His orders were to capture the ubir in Osaka and return

him to Savar, who would, with a few older *venari,* put him in a cell. Rhapta had cells deep underground to hold prisoners, but it was mainly used for ubir as they were Rhapta's biggest enemy.

How could he bring in his own brother? The brother who had cared for him when he fell from the baobab trees? The brother who bought him *guakal* when he had no money? Or the brother whose calming presence was there for him the night he had been tapped as a *venari*? How ironic was it that Amir would have to be taken in by the same boy he spent the majority of his life caring for?

Zaid's stomach twisted.

As he remembered the times Amir had cared for him, he remembered the times he wasn't there too. All the times he had come home only to anger their mother or to speak against the Elders. The more Zaid thought about it, Amir had *abandoned* him. Nobody had forced him to leave Rhapta to become an ubir. The choice was his and his alone. He had decided to kill another living being just to escape the city over staying with his brother and mother.

Anger started to boil in Zaid's stomach. How dare he do this to him! He stood from his seat and started walking back the way he had come.

He opened his senses again and found the shattered Aura in moments. Across the street and down another, he walked. With each step, bitter hatred choked him. He had never done anything to deserve this. He had gone to school and loved his family and even accepted his appointment as one of the *venari* with grace. He *never* deserved what Amir did to him when he left.

Moving into a full sprint, Zaid moved faster than the eye could see. As he passed by, wind ruffled the humans' hair, and they thought a strong breeze danced down the street. But Zaid followed the Aura and within minutes was in a dark alley.

Amir was there, walking slowly toward the back of the alley, and Zaid saw why. A young girl cowered at the back, watching the menacing face of his brother come closer. He saw Amir had a short, blunt knife in one hand and realized what he had meant to do.

Hot rage pooled in his chest as Amir whirled to see him. His eyes widened momentarily, but he never got to scream as Zaid punched him right in the nose.

CHAPTER 13
COMPOUNDING UNCERTAINTY

Zaid couldn't breathe. Not that he didn't want to, or that his airway was blocked off. He just wasn't allowed to. The body could only last a few minutes at most without oxygen, he would pass out first, of course, but he didn't know if the ubir's compulsion would last in unconsciousness.

He was rooted to the floor, his lungs burning, and he had several broken ribs. Years of training had him focusing his mind and pushing the pain someplace far away. Once his own mind was quiet again, he found where the ubir's anchor was buried deep. He started tugging and pulling at it, but it was as if roots were starting to form and burrowed deeper.

His lungs were on fire. From his spot on the floor, he could see the dark sheen of one of his daggers laying on the nearest bed. If only he could move.

He went slower this time, trying to pry mental fingers under the lip of the anchor, trying to wedge it out. The ubir's attention was firmly on the compulsion now that he wasn't distracted by Zaid's punches. That's what he needed, something to distract—

As if a literal miracle was sent from the sky, a body plummeted past the window, screaming the whole way down only to end in silence as it thudded to the ground.

The ubir's attention was diverted for a split second by the sound. That's all Zaid needed to mentally shove himself under the anchor and rip it free. The compulsion eddied out of him like water down a drain, and he sucked in a long breath.

As the ubir realized what he had done, Zaid didn't give him a chance to sink the anchor in again. Using one knee to stand, he reached over in one fluid motion, grabbed the dagger off the bed, and plunged it upward into the ubir's chest.

A faint grunt could be heard before Zaid heard the ubir's heartbeat come to an immediate halt. The Aura faded last like mist dispersing in the dawn. It was always the last to go.

The body fell to the floor, and Zaid stood up. His brother's face flashed in his mind, and he almost retched. He would rather be under compulsion a thousand times over than relive that memory, so he buried it again like he always did.

He limped over to the balcony and stepped out. It was truly only meant for show as it barely protruded out of the wall. They all looked to be like that. The room was indeed on the second floor, almost in the corner looking out onto the lake. To the right was a small copse of trees lining the edge of the building, and as he peered down, he could see a prone form lying in the grass.

Zaid's ribs were aching, and blood dripped down his face. He needed to get Kinza and get out. They would have to come back for the other ubir later. He was just about to go back inside when he heard voices up on the roof.

Looking up, he was confused to see silky black hair drifting in the breeze up above. The back of Kinza's head and torso came into view as she backed up against the low wall around the lip of the roof.

"Kinza!" he shouted, trying to get her attention, but his voice was hoarse, and it came out quieter than he intended. What was she doing?

He suddenly realized who was on the ground; it must have been the ubir Ghassan. But where was the last one? He looked up again and saw that Kinza was backing up against the wall, hands slightly raised.

No. Basma must have been up there with her, and Kinza had nowhere to run. If she fell, she was too far over for him to catch her. "Kinza!" he yelled again. She must have heard him this time because she turned her head in his direction. But as she did so, Zaid saw a slender leg come into view, extended in Kinza's direction. She tried to twist to avoid the blow, but she was already backed against the wall, and the motion caused her to flip over and plummet down the side of the building.

"Kin—No!" Zaid yelled. He watched her body drop down to fall toward Ghassan's form on the ground within the trees. A sick feeling of dread came over him when he didn't see any movement from between the trees.

He looked up and saw the slight figure of Basma standing on the roof's edge. He couldn't quite make out her expression, but when she noticed him, she slipped away from the edge and out of sight.

A breath later, he was running out of the room.

KINZA SPAT OUT A LEAF. Brambles tangled in her hair, and she crawled out of the bush and looked around.

She was standing by a line of trees on the other side of the parking lot, close to the main road, probably a quarter-mile from the hotel.

A quarter-mile from the hotel.

Just moments ago, she had watched the ubir fall off the roof. She had turned around, intending to go back inside, when she found a slender woman standing just behind her. The woman had to be no more than a few years older than her at most, but she had the same unfocused eyes that the man had. A feral grin had slid across her face at Kinza's blatant fear, and she realized this must have been one of the other ubir.

Kinza had tried pleading with her, but the woman only stalked closer, each step as graceful as a dancer. When she had kicked out, Kinza tried to avoid it, but the woman was too fast. Kinza fumbled and flipped backward over the edge of the roof, stomach-lurching into her throat.

Freefalling was not pleasant, but neither was landing in a bush a quarter-mile away. One second she had been falling, and the next, she had thumped to the ground within the brambles, just hard enough to knock the breath out of her.

Kinza examined her arms and legs, nothing felt broken, but the bewildering feeling of being somewhere she physically couldn't be had her mind reeling. She started walking back into the parking lot toward the truck. She was pulling leaves from her hair and rubbing the hip she had landed on. There would be a bruise for sure.

"Kinza!" a deep voice shouted. It startled her so much she jumped, thinking it was another ubir. She relaxed when she saw it was Zaid and Haris running toward her from the other side of the lot. Zaid obviously arrived much quicker and grabbed her by the shoulders, shaking her gently. "Are you injured?" he asked. He didn't bother waiting for an answer and started patting down her arms and sides. Kinza saw that he was way worse than she was. Blood ran down his nose, a long scrape was slowly being knit together along his jawline, and one eye was half swollen shut. It looked like he had been in a brawl.

"Uhh…"

"Why did you come all the way over here? And why are you wearing my sweatshirt?" he fired off the questions.

"I didn't," was all she said.

"You didn't? Didn't what?" He was clearly distracted by checking for injuries. She tried to swat him away, but it was no use. Haris showed up wheezing and put both hands on his knees.

"I…" He took a breath. "I despise you both right now." He took another gulp. "Kinza, why did you come over here after you fell?"

"I didn't."

"What do you mean you didn't?" Zaid asked after deeming her whole and uninjured.

"I mean I didn't go anywhere. I was on the roof, and then I fell but landed over here in that bush." She pointed back toward the unlucky bush, looking as if it had been mashed into the ground. Sirens wailed far away but were getting closer.

"What?" Haris said at the same time as Zaid said, "We have to go." He grabbed her wrist and started pulling her back to the truck.

"What about that woman?" Kinza asked, and then quieter, "Zaid, you can let go. I can walk."

"She got away, but we need to leave. I don't want to get caught up in the police, and Basma could come back."

"Who is Basma?" Haris asked.

"Zaid, let go," Kinza said.

He kept walking to the truck, Kinza in tow. "Something is definitely going on if you have a teleportation ability, so I need to talk to Tahir as soon as we get back to Rhapta."

"Teleportation?!" Kinza and Haris both said. Kinza dug her feet into the ground, causing Zaid to stop and look at her. He dropped her wrist as if he hadn't realized he was still hanging onto her.

"Yes, it's an ability, but an extremely rare one."

"I'm confused," Haris said, and if he was confused, Kinza was sure to be. "So you do have abilities? I thought you said she had no Aura?"

"She doesn't, and yeah, at least two abilities, and she heals like Anunnaki." He got in the truck, still talking. "Tahir, my mentor, will know what to do. He must have known something otherwise, they wouldn't have given me your name. There might have been a mistake though if he thought you were ubir."

"Wait, go back to the teleportation part," Kinza said. She got into the front seat and Haris in the back.

"I didn't know that teleportation was an ability," Haris piped in. "What's the point of portals then?"

"Well, they're not—" Zaid started, but Kinza cut him off.

"So I just teleported?! I didn't even *do* anything! It just happened."

"You might have just—" Zaid started again.

"I've known about quite a few abilities, but that is a bit of a stretch..." Haris said.

"And how was landing in a bush helpful? I didn't even choose to—" Kinza started.

"Shut up!" Zaid yelled. "Both of you, be quiet until we get back to the apartment." He took a deep breath, and Kinza realized, again, how bad he looked. "Please, just let me think, and when we get back, we can talk about it."

Kinza had half a mind to snap at him that she wasn't a child that needed to be shushed. But the exhausted look on his face had her deciding to wait.

They sat in silence on the way back, the whole time Kinza watched the tiny scrapes on her hands from the bush heal faster than should be possible. The sight made her uneasy, but if what Zaid had said was true, then healing scrapes would be the least of her worries.

WHEN THEY GOT BACK to the apartment, Zaid immediately passed out on one of the beds.

"So much for talking about it," Kinza said. "What if that other ubir, Basma, followed us?" she asked and peered out of the blinds to the beach farther out.

"I'm sure Zaid isn't entirely worried about her. It's one ubir, and from what he said, her ability was more along the lines of acrobatics or movement, nothing that he can't handle."

The thought of that woman still out there didn't make her feel any better. She took off Zaid's hoodie and gently shook off the remaining leaves before placing it back in the duffle bag he had dropped by the door. She was careful not to touch the *laqueus* as she did so.

"What happened to Zaid then? He looked like he had been run over by a herd of rhinos."

"After you went inside, which I'm still mad at you for, by the way," he said pointedly, "I waited outside the truck for one of you to come back. Honestly, I was about to go after you, but Zaid came sprinting out the front door and around the hotel to the side by the lake. He was only there for a second and then came to the truck, and yeah, he looked pretty gnarly. He said he had killed one of the ubir, saw another fall off the roof, and then saw *you* fall off the roof. He ran outside, and you weren't there."

"There were a ton of people swarming around by that time. You guys caused a bit of a commotion. So he came back to the truck and started yelling at me for letting you leave, and then we saw you come out of the trees." Haris seemed both intrigued and annoyed. She was sure it was an emotion only he could pull off.

Kinza rubbed at her arms. Everything felt off-kilter and unsteady, and she wanted some sort of solid ground in her life at that moment. She had life neatly planned out a few days ago, and now she wasn't sure of anything. It was yet another moment she wished her parents were with her. Even if they didn't have the answers, they would have held her and told her it would be all right.

She curled up on a worn sofa sitting in the living room right off the kitchen. "I don't understand. So I am Anunnaki then?"

Haris sat sideways on an armchair, which happened to be the only other piece of furniture in the room. "That's the strange part, it's like you are, and you aren't. You have the mark, but no Aura apparently, but you do have the healing, but your family isn't Anunnaki. You weren't adopted, were you?"

Kinza shook her head and smiled, "No, I look just like my dad. There's literally no way."

"Hmm, well, scratch that theory. But you do have at least one ability that I've literally never heard of. Zaid said you had another?"

"I, um, may have exploded a couple of rooms," she mumbled. For some reason, admitting that one might have supernatural abilities was embarrassing.

"You....what?" Haris asked.

She sighed. "When Zaid came to kidnap me the first time, I was asleep, or dreaming really, and I woke up from a white light and an explosion. I thought *he* had exploded my room somehow, but it had thrown him into the living room. And then again, when we had stopped for gas one day, this ninja assassin-looking man attacked me, and I did it again in the bathroom. It was big enough to rip a hole through the wall."

Haris's eyebrows went to his hairline. "Ninja assassin? You were going to casually just throw that in there?"

"Yeah, forgot to mention that part. I'm being followed by a couple of assassins, and Zaid doesn't know who they are but says they are Anunnaki."

"You have a strange life," he said, almost as if he was morbidly fascinated by her being attacked. "Well, I don't know what to make of it. It's like you're Anunnaki... but not."

"Could I be half or something?"

He shook his head, sending a few bright red strands across his forehead. "No, we do know that for sure. Even if an Anunnaki had a child with a human, they will either be human or Anunnaki; never both. Although the gene tends to be recessive for some reason, so more likely human."

"Do you think Zaid still thinks I'm an ubir?" she asked. The ever-present thought of "losing" her trial in Rhapta kept reminding her she wasn't in the clear.

Haris smiled softly, "Yeah, I think he knows that you're not. Despite the obvious trait of rule-breaking you apparently have." He yawned. "All right, I'm in desperate need of sleep. Wake me up if someone comes to kill you." He headed toward the unoccupied room. "On second thought, let me sleep and wake Zaid up."

Kinza laughed. "Will do."

CHAPTER 14

TURNING TIDES

Kinza dozed on the couch for a few hours, not really sleeping. Eventually, the noise of the tv sounded more appealing than trying to wrangle her thoughts. There was only cable, so she let the local evening news play. The reporter announced two murders at a resort and hotel nearby. The familiar image of the hotel appeared on screen, surrounded by several police cars and an ambulance. She almost felt guilty as the reporter said the perpetrators had not been caught, only vague images provided and no suspects at the moment.

Haris came back out yawning and immediately went into the kitchen. The sound of pots and pans and boiling water filled the room. It did little to assuage the unease she felt every time the reporter mentioned the word "murder" or "investigation." The air in the apartment started to feel stifling.

The glass door unlocked easily as she slid it open and stepped out onto the balcony. There were a couple of plastic chairs and a tiny table. She curled up on one of the chairs and let the cool breeze distract her.

Whenever she was upset, Grams would tell her to let herself feel her emotions and not to hide from them. But right now, they made her sick. Everything felt unsteady, as if she were walking through a dream, and the floor kept buckling. She looked down at her healed hands. What was she? How could she go back to Grams now? What would she tell her? Those thoughts only made her stomach churn more.

The glass door slid open, and a tall figure stepped out. Kinza tucked her hands under her arms and glanced at Zaid. He looked monumentally better than he had earlier, the cuts on his face gone, the blood wiped away. He had changed his clothes as well and no longer looked like he had been in a brawl.

"Well, you're looking better," she mumbled. She didn't know why but she was nervous to talk to him.

He just looked at her, eyes roaming over her arms and legs before he sat down in silence. She had the urge to snap that she was fine but held it back. They stayed like that for a while, looking out at the dark beach on the other side of the street. A few people walked along the shore, cell phones out for the light. The sound of the water gently lapping reached them all the way up on the balcony.

"Do you want to call your grandmother?" Zaid asked suddenly. She looked over to him, expecting to see some smirk or sarcastic expression, but all he did was pull a cell phone out of his pocket and hold it out to her. The light from the apartment lit up the side of the screen and his outstretched hand.

She couldn't help but stare at it. After two days of wanting nothing more, she couldn't bring herself to take it. "I don't know what I would say to her." She turned back to the water, and out of the corner of her eye, she saw him hesitate and then tuck it back in his pocket. The thought of talking to Grams was comforting, but the idea of trying to explain what was happening made her more nauseous and exhausted. There was nothing she could say that would ease Grams' fears about her safety. Maybe she would wait to call her, even if it made her feel like a coward.

"Wouldn't she want to know you are all right?" he asked.

She snorted. "Oh, now he cares," she said and crossed her arms tighter.

He didn't answer, just shook his head and sat there. They were quiet for a few more minutes, and she almost forgot he was there. He was just so *still*. It was like sitting next to a massive, dark statue. She mentally replaced his head with a jackal and could see him as Anubis, the ancient Egyptian god of the underworld. For a moment, it made her feel small sitting next to him.

She almost started to feel guilty. It's not like she wanted to fight with him; it was more of a reflex at this point. He had tried to look out for her, but she was throwing it back in his face. Another of Gram's million lessons berated her mind about treating people the right way... or something like that. She inhaled, ready to apologize, but Zaid cut her off.

"I know you don't want to go, but I still think it's a good idea to go to Rhapta. There is definitely something going on, and my mentor, Tahir, will help you. There must have been some mistake, but he can figure out what exactly you are." *What* she was, as if she wasn't human.

"You don't think they'll accuse me of being an ubir and have me killed?" she asked, looking at the streetlight reflecting on the water.

"I won't let them kill you," he said. The statement was so contradictory to the last few days she had to look at him, suspicious of the promise. "And I honestly don't think your trial would last more than five minutes. It's clear you're not ubir; just something else." Dark eyes glanced toward her and held steady. His face held nothing other than honesty, and she relaxed. He looked at her a moment longer, causing her cheeks to heat before he looked away abruptly.

Kinza cleared her throat. "So about this teleportation—"

"We should probably talk about—" he said at the same time. An awkward chuckle rumbled in his chest. "Yeah, we should talk about these abilities of yours. They are clearly dangerous, and we need to see if you have even an ounce of control. I don't want to be exploded in my sleep before we get there."

Kinza rolled her eyes. "Well, what about babies? How do little kids have any control over their abilities?"

"Young children don't have their abilities yet," he said, leaning forward, elbows resting on his knees. "Anunnaki come into their abilities about their tenth year. Very few come in before that and even less after that. Up until that time, we are taught a certain level of mental and emotional control, so when the abilities do come, we are somewhat ready."

"Are you saying—"

Zaid held up a hand. "I'm not saying you are mentally and emotionally unstable, but yes, it is true that humans don't train their children for non-existent responsibilities like this."

She laced and unlaced her fingers a moment, thinking. "When did you get yours?"

"When I was eleven," he said, grimacing. "It's almost unheard of to get them so late, but they did come eventually, I guess."

"So it would be unlikely that someone would develop abilities at eighteen..."

"It's never happened," he said, glancing in her direction. "There are very, very few Anunnaki that don't develop any abilities, but they are usually shunned or forced to the outskirts of the city."

"That's... sad. Does everyone have two?" Kinza asked.

"No, most have one, a much smaller group has two, and one of the Elders has three. Never more than that."

"We're kinda special then, huh?" she said, grinning and waggling her eyebrows at him. He looked away, but she swore she saw him hold back a smile.

"We're just lucky, that's all." He heaved a sigh and sat back. "For the time being, we should at least narrow down what yours are and make sure you don't kill anyone with them. We know you have the teleportation now. Can't you remember what happened when you did it?"

Kinza tilted her head to the side, humming as she thought. It was a gesture she knew she had picked up from her mother. "Not really. I just remember falling, and of course, panicking as I was falling, thinking I was going to break every bone in my body. And then I twisted and just landed in that bush."

"Ah, but you were panicked, though?"

"Well, yeah? I was falling? You would be, too."

"That was most likely what triggered it," he said, ignoring her tone. "Strong emotions tend to bring out abilities. And you said you twisted? How?"

"I don't know. I was flailing about like a falling squirrel. I'm not sure how to recreate that one." She continued a little louder when Zaid started to stand. The hell if she would let him throw her over the balcony. "And I don't think that one is going to hurt anyone other than myself. Maybe we should focus on the exploding thing instead."

He sat back down, looking almost forlorn at the missed opportunity. "Hmm, yes, I suppose you are right. You've... exploded twice now, correct?"

She nodded.

He looked at her expectantly. "Well, explain," he said, as if it should be obvious.

Kinza huffed and thought again. "The first time I was having a nightmare, and I was scared and then, I guess, did it in my sleep. And then I woke up, and everything was destroyed, and a maniac was in my living room."

Zaid glared at her under heavy-lidded eyes but asked, confused, "A nightmare? Tell me about it."

She chewed on her lip before she spoke. "I had it for a week, every night. I would be walking through a forest or a jungle, and then there would be this totem pole with a skull and stuff, and then some kind of... barrier? From there, it always changed. But I would always go through and enter this city with massive buildings, and it would be totally silent. This last time I walked until I was in the center, by some sort of statue, and then a bunch of ancient warrior-looking dudes in red paint showed up. They were all just about to attack me when I woke up."

When Zaid didn't respond, she looked over and barked a laugh. The incredulous look on his face was either because he thought she was truly crazy or he knew what the nightmare meant. "*That* would be Rhapta," he said, confirming it was the latter.

"Huh. Well, what does it mean?"

"I have literally not a single clue, but that is definitely it. We can add that to the list of things to figure out when we get there. So you were afraid again, and then... exploded. It seems we have a pattern."

"It was the same in the gas station," Kinza replied. She felt a slight excitement at the prospect of understanding *something*. "That assassin came in and was literally an inch from carving me in half, and the light exploded." She paused before saying, "What exactly is that light? Is that part of the explosion?" It was starting to get chilly outside, and she rubbed her arms.

"Mmm," he hummed. "I don't know. What I do know is

that you have two very powerful abilities that are tied to your emotions, particularly fear. Try to stay as neutral as possible, at least until we get to Rhapta."

"How am I supposed to do that when you are running off, getting yourself into fights, and I have to graciously come and rescue you?" she asked with a sly grin.

Zaid looked at her with a bewildered expression. "Excuse me? If that brain of yours remembered correctly, I told you to stay in the truck. I needed no rescuing, and you did nothing to help."

Kinza gasped in mockery, "How dare you? I took on two of the ubir while you were flirting with the other one."

"*Flirting?*" Zaid asked, going up an octave. His mouth pulled into a half-grin that gave her what she refused to admit were butterflies. "You arrogant—"

Zaid was cut off by the glass door sliding open. Haris's pale face poked out. "Are you two going to eat any of this? It's getting cold, and I'm still hungry."

Kinza stifled a giggle at how quickly Zaid's face melted into a neutral expression. "I think I'm heading to bed. You two eat up."

"Hey," Zaid said over his shoulder as she was stepping inside. "We are leaving early to get to the portal. Be awake at five."

Kinza just rolled her eyes. "Yes, your highness."

Zaid spent the next five minutes berating himself. He had completely lost focus of his entire surroundings, twice, in one conversation with Kinza. Years as *venari* had him noting all movement, heartbeats, and nearest exits at all times. He realized how sad she had looked, not even wanting to call her family. A stab of guilt had pierced him and then when she looked at him, really looked at him, he practically stopped breathing and nearly forgot his name for a moment. Maybe it was something about those eyes...

Zaid groaned and blamed his lapse in attention on delayed healing or something like that. He desperately wanted to get back to Rhapta to find out what was going on. He would need to come back afterward to take care of the last ubir. The street down below was quiet now, no sign of Basma. She had probably fled into hiding. She was much less of a threat now that she was alone, and he wasn't too worried about her either.

The only danger now was those damned assassins. As far as he knew, Rhapta didn't send assassins out like that. The Elders that focused on human societies would only have someone killed in absolute extreme situations. Hakim, the Grand Elder, has only had two visions in his entire lifetime that required such an irreversible action. Generally, they were visions of the end of times or some sort of societal collapse at one person's existence. As soon as the person was killed, Hakim's visions would subside back to peace.

They never sent assassins on other Anunnaki, though. There was no point. If an Anunnaki was a threat and had left the city, they would be an ubir, and it was the *venari's* job to capture them. Why send both?

Too many possibilities swirled in his mind. He went back into the warmth of the apartment, firmly locking the door behind him. Haris sat on the couch with a pot of now-cold spaghetti in his lap. How he could eat so much was truly one of life's greater mysteries. The last time Zaid ate was early that morning before he had found Kinza at the house in the woods. Realistically he could go another two days, but he would probably just wait until he got back to Rhapta. Even after so long of mingling in human society, there wasn't much that he had the stomach for.

"Headed back to my house in the morning then?" Haris said, not looking over as Zaid sat in the armchair. A reporter recycled the same story he knew would be playing for hours. The bodies found at the resort, a vague description of him and Kinza, and no other suspects. He sighed. Savar would be displeased.

"Yes. I want to get to Rhapta as quickly as possible. I'll come back for Basma after I figure out what is going on with the girl." He looked over at Haris. "You'll be all right until I get back?"

Haris nodded absentmindedly, looking into the pot. "Yeah, not worried about that one." Zaid waited for him to continue. He had known Haris long enough to know when there was something on his mind. Surprisingly, despite the incessant joking around, the occasional bright spot of wisdom would show itself. "Zaid." He paused again, "have you given thought to the prophecy at all? You know the one I'm talking about."

Zaid listened for Kinza's heartbeat in the other room. It had slowed into the deep rhythms of sleep. When he was satisfied she couldn't hear them, he responded, "Haris, I trust in the Elders, but even I know a centuries-long ploy by a government to keep people in line when I see one. It's not real."

"Then what do you make of an eighteen-year-old Anunnaki with budding abilities living in Chicago and a swarm of assassins after her? Other *venari* talk of the rebel groups that live in Rhapta, the ones that abhor the Elders' grip on the city and the Grand Elder's prophecies. You don't think someone from one of those groups would want *her* dead?"

Zaid shook his head. "Savar has always given *venari* the right people to bring in. If anything, I can talk with Ishar. He would know why she exists outside of the city. It's probably just a special ability of hers... handy, but just an ability."

Haris leaned back and grinned at him. "Ah, my dear friend," he mocked. "Are we a little afraid of destiny? I would think the supernatural beings living in a hidden city in the middle of Tanzania would have a little more faith than that." His chastisement sounded eerily like Zaid's mother.

Zaid didn't answer; he was done with this conversation. He hoped Haris would take the hint and shut up.

They watched tv for ten minutes before Haris got up. "All right, I need to sleep. You can have the couch. Wake me up in the morning." He went to walk down the hall, but turned back. "Oh, and was that you *flirting* with destiny on my balcony?" He nodded toward the sliding door. "*Tsk, tsk.* Careful, Zaid, you almost looked happy."

His lanky form had entered the bedroom before Zaid got a chance to throw his dagger.

CHAPTER 15

NO TURNING BACK

Kinza felt like she was in heaven. The smell of fresh-brewed coffee wafted around the interior of the truck. Haris had forced Zaid to stop at a gas station to grab breakfast before they headed back to his house. He went in as he was the only one who wasn't a wanted suspect in a murder investigation, but all thoughts of dead bodies left Kinza's mind when he came back out with three coffees and a stack of steaming breakfast sandwiches.

"Did you buy all of them?" she asked around a mouthful of egg and biscuit that tasted vaguely of cardboard. She ate three.

Haris shrugged in the backseat. "Zaid said he was buying."

"No," Zaid said. "You took my card and left." He sipped one of the coffees but didn't touch the sandwiches. The light of morning was just reaching over the tops of the houses as they drove through the streets to the other side of town. Kinza tugged down the sleeves of the sweater Haris had lent her. The morning chill had permeated the cab of the truck. It was almost peaceful watching the sunrise over the lake as they passed it by, but knowing the world was tainted with things like the ubir made it hard to enjoy. She tried anyway.

The old hotel was quiet when they pulled into the parking lot. It was still too early for checkout, and guests slept soundly in their rooms. They pulled around back this time, closer to Haris' house.

Zaid and Kinza followed Haris as he trumped through the short path into the woods. The quaint little cottage appeared, and Kinza noticed the "Groundkeeper's Lodge" sign that sat to the left of the door. Haris pushed the door open as it was still unlocked and stepped through, Zaid behind him. As Kinza followed them, she caught sight of the swirling carving on the side of the doorframe that she saw last time. It suddenly clicked where she had seen it before.

"We have this at my house too!" she exclaimed. It was the same design of overlapping infinity symbols.

Haris and Zaid looked back at her from the living room. It was still destroyed, and Haris had started righting furniture and picking up papers. "That's unlikely, my friend. It's the mark of the Ummanu. We all have it on our doors so the *venari* can recognize us." He turned back to righting furniture.

"What?" Kinza asked dumbly, still standing in the doorway. Zaid walked over and stood close.

"This is on the door of your house?" he asked.

"Yes," she said, looking at it.

"You're sure?" he asked, ducking his head down to her level.

"Yes," she snapped this time. "I've lived there my whole life. I could draw it in my sleep."

"Then either someone in your family was or is Ummanu, or you are living in the old house of one." He turned to Haris, "Are there any portals in Chicago?"

There goes the scrap of peace I had this morning, Kinza thought to herself. Was Grams Ummanu, and she never knew it? Were her parents? At this point, she didn't know what to think.

Kinza closed the door and stepped inside. "My grandma has lived in that house since she was a little girl, so it's been in our family for a long time."

Half of a broken lamp fell to the ground and shattered. Haris, holding the other half, sighed. "Not that I'm aware of. There are Ummanu that don't directly watch over portals, but they are usually relatives of the ones who do and live close by. It would be unusual for an Ummanu to live solitarily away from the portals and without connection to Rhapta, but it wouldn't be unheard of. That might explain a few things, actually," he said, looking toward Kinza.

"It would?" she and Zaid asked in unison. He had started righting things again, doing so several times faster than what she and Haris could do in an hour. In a matter of moments, the cushions were back on the couch, the glass swept off the floor, the remaining furniture in its correct position, and papers stacked neatly on the kitchen table Kinza could see just around the corner.

"Well... I shouldn't say 'explain,' but it would show that you have *some* connection to the Anunnaki. Do your parents have a large collection of crystals or anything like that?"

Kinza picked at the cuticle on her thumb. "My parents died a long time ago. I just live with my grandma. And no, she doesn't have crystals or anything that I know of."

"But she does have that Deathstone," Zaid's deep voice echoed from the kitchen. The sound of plates being put back sounded so *mundane* to her.

Haris stood and truly looked at her this time. "Kinza, it's very likely your grandmother is Ummanu then. She never mentioned Rhapta or Anunnaki at all? Even as a bedtime story or a myth?"

Kinza just shook her head. She didn't want to talk about it anymore. Zaid had come back into the living room and glanced toward her face. "Portal still good?" he asked, abruptly changing the subject.

"Yeah, they can't actually do anything to it. Are you ready to go?" Haris asked.

Kinza looked toward Zaid, and he nodded. "Okay then, follow me." The two of them trailed behind Haris to the first door in the hallway. It led down a rickety staircase into the basement. Kinza half expected there to be a giant glowing circle sitting down there in the dark, but the room was well-kept and seemingly devoid of obvious portals. Wooden racks lined two walls, filled with hundreds of crystals of different sizes and colors, all laid out neatly. There was a row of crystals sitting on the floor in front of one of the walls. The third wall held what looked like a back storage room, and against the fourth wall sat a washer and dryer.

"Laundry in the morning and portal hopping in the afternoon?" she asked. Zaid turned to glare at her, but Haris gave a wry grin.

"Yes, but I'm not the one doing the hopping," Haris said.

"Ummanu don't ever go through?" she asked.

Haris shrugged. "We don't need to. It's really just for *venari* to travel back and forth to Rhapta, and sometimes to other cities around the world. Other than that, the portals don't get much use."

"Almost seems like a waste," Kinza said more to herself. If she had known a portal to just about any country around the world lay in upstate Michigan, she and her parents could have gone on so many vacations. Just pop on over to Morocco for a weekend and home in time for Sunday dinner with Grams. She tucked that thought away into the pile of things she wouldn't ever get a chance to do with her parents.

While Haris dug around the shelves grabbing various crystals, Zaid turned to her. "This probably will be unpleasant the first time, but it won't hurt you."

"Unpleasant how?" she asked. Was she going to come out the other side missing limbs?

"Just don't puke on me," he said and turned back to Haris, who was lining up his crystals on the floor in a random pattern perpendicular to the other line across the room.

"So where is this portal then? Do you keep it in a box or something?"

"It's actually all around us, pretty much everywhere the house sits. I just keep the crystals down here."

"What are they for?"

Haris looked up and grinned at her, his brown eyes nearly black in the dim lighting. "They just open the door." As he said it, he placed the last crystal at the end of the line. Almost immediately, the air started to shimmer along the length of them, rising up to the ceiling, almost like heat waves wafting up. Kinza stepped forward to get a better look, but it was no warmer as she got closer. It truly did look like a mirage in the desert or a rippling curtain. At first, she could see right through it to the other side of the room, but after a moment, she swore she could see blue sky and the interior of a house. The image came in and out of focus, making her blink, trying to see better.

Zaid stepped up beside her, "Remember what I said about puking," he muttered, slinging his duffel back over his shoulder.

"Well, Kinza. It's been a pleasure, and I'm sure I'll be seeing you again soon," he said. He stood leaning against one wall of shelves, arms crossed.

"Wait, you're not coming with us?" she asked. "What about that other ubir? What if she comes back?"

"That one won't be a problem. She is probably long gone for now, expecting other *venari* to show up," Haris said.

"But—" she started.

"Don't worry, he'll be fine," Zaid said, looking into the portal. "Let's go," he said and, without looking at her, stepped over the line of crystals into the shimmering wall and vanished.

Kinza gasped.

"On your way now, little anomaly," Haris said, coming over to shoo her into the portal.

She held her breath and cringed as she stepped through.

KINZA WAS IMMEDIATELY HIT with a wave of nausea, and it felt like a thousand needles prickled across her skin. They were in an empty room with one open window that looked out on a sunlit street. A plain door sat to one side that led out; she immediately ran for the door, wrenching it open. Kinza didn't even look at her surroundings and vomited along the side of the house, emptying her beloved breakfast to the last drop.

From back inside the room, a woman was yelling in another language, and Zaid's voice rumbled in answer in the same language. When Kinza was done, she wiped her mouth on the back of her sleeve and stepped back inside. She hadn't seen the hallway on the other side of the room. A woman in a t-shirt and a wrap skirt stood in the hall waving in Kinza's direction while yelling at Zaid. From the placating hand motions she was doing, she could guess that the woman was angry she had just vomited outside her house.

"Sorry," Kinza said, feeling guilty, not knowing if the woman understood her.

"Ach! Anunnaki come in and out of my home like a hotel," she said in English. "And who is this? A new *venari*?" She laughed, bright and sharp. "She looks like you did the first time you came through here. Get her cleaned up!" she shouted the last part at Zaid and left back down the hallway, deeper into the house.

Zaid just shook his head and shouted something down the hall at her. "Come on," he said to Kinza and steered her back out into the street. She wabbled a bit when she got outside, the wave of heat a sharp contrast to the chilly morning in Michigan. Zaid grabbed her under her upper arm and kept her from falling over.

"Thanks," she mumbled.

He sighed. "At least you didn't puke on me. Let's go. I'm guessing you want food and clothing?"

She nodded vigorously, her mood brightening at the prospect. She felt like she was dreaming as she looked at her surroundings in full now. Gone was the little cottage by Lake Michigan, replaced by a bustling town and the midday sun beating down on her head. Sweat started to bead on the back of her neck.

Kinza followed Zaid down the street, past one-story houses similar to the one they just left. People walked every which way shouting and laughing, cars honking as they swerved around pedestrians. They soon came out to a larger intersection of streets, most of which looked to be lined with stores, restaurants, and businesses, each with doors and windows wide open to let the breeze in.

"Where are we?" she asked finally. It was already way too warm for her sweater, so she took it off. It smelled of vomit anyway. Thankfully she was wearing a tank top underneath.

"Moshi, a town about an hour's drive from Mount Kiliman-jaro," he said ahead of her. She was glad for once he was so large, the chances of losing him in the swarms of people was low.

"And that woman back there was Ummanu then?" she asked. A vendor to one side was selling fruit and what looked like meat on a stick. Her mouth started to water now that her stomach was empty again.

"Yes, Bahati is the Ummanu to the portal closest to Rhapta. Her family has held it for generations, and with it being the closest, it tends to get the most activity. Don't worry, she yells at me every time. It's almost like a tradition," he said. He strode down the street until he found what he was looking for. An ATM sat squished between two buildings. After inserting his card and punching a few numbers, the machine spat out a stack of bills she didn't recognize.

"What language was she speaking?"

"Swahili, most people speak that or English here," he said, turning back down the street. His long stride had her half jogging to keep up. She desperately needed water now.

"You speak Swahili?" she asked twisting out of the way of a group of men carrying boxes.

"I speak seventeen languages fluently and five passably. So yes."

Kinza's mouth popped open. Mitra's voice barreled into her mind like an unwelcome fairy on her shoulder. *So he's attractive* and *hella smart?* Kinza batted the thought away. She said nothing as she followed him down the street. Just as she was about to start complaining of heatstroke, he turned into a small open-air shop. Fans blew from every corner, instantly cooling her sweltering skin. Racks of clothing, toiletries, and several coolers with drinks were crammed into the small space.

"Here," Zaid said, pointing around them. "Get what you need."

Kinza didn't need him to tell her twice. She quickly grabbed two bottles of water, a pack of disinfectant wipes, deodorant, toothbrush and toothpaste, a pair of dark green flowy pants that cinched at the ankles, and a canvas backpack, throwing it all up on the counter. Zaid paid, and the man behind the counter showed her to a small dressing room in the back where she could change. Five minutes later, she stepped out feeling a million times better.

It had been days since she had straightened her hair, and with the hell it had been through, the edges were starting to curl. She decided that pulling it back into a low ponytail was as good as it would get for the time being. She stuffed the sweater into a garbage bin in the corner and mentally promised to buy Haris another one.

Chugging the first bottle of water, she handed the second to Zaid. He nodded and downed his as well. "All right, it's early afternoon here. If we hurry, we have time to get you food, and then we'll head toward the mountain."

"How long until we actually get to the city?" she asked, squinting into the sunlight.

"It's about a forty-five-minute drive and then a two-hour walk to the barrier. So we'll probably get there later in the evening, but that's fine."

She followed him down the street again, staying close to his back. Kinza was pretty sure she would have gotten run over several times by now, but Zaid moved throughout the busy street like water around a rock, meandering them both out of the way of cars, bikes, and pedestrians. He didn't go far before entering an open-air restaurant. All the tables inside were occupied, so they sat outside under a large awning. They didn't have to wait long until a man came over and took their order and deposited two Cokes on the table.

When he was gone, Kinza leaned back in the chair, letting the gentle breeze wrap over her shoulder. It was much better out of the sun. "Do you ever just go on vacation?" she asked abruptly.

Zaid mirrored her position on the other side of the table. "There is no time," he said. "There are more and more ubir every day and not enough *venari* to capture them."

"Oh," she said lamely.

Zaid sat up and put his forearms on the table. "But occasionally, I'll take longer on a mission when it's in nice places," he said with a half-smile.

"Really?" she asked. "Like where?"

"A few places. Greece, Machu Pichu, Bali, Nebraska—"

"*Nebraska?!*" she asked incredulously. "What about Nebraska screams 'vacation' to you?"

Zaid considered her with lowered eyebrows as if debating whether or not to tell her. Finally, he looked around and said, "I saw a lot of horses there. I liked to watch them." He looked everywhere but at her.

"That is so... adorable," she said, erupting into a fit of laughter. Zaid looked like he regretted telling her. "Did you ride one?"

"No." He looked affronted. "I'm not stupid enough to get *on* one of those things. I'm not actually invincible, you know."

It was Kinza's turn to eye him. "You had me fooled." He glanced at her and then away, and a ghost of a smile appeared. "I wanted to go to China when I was younger," she said, hoping she didn't embarrass him *too* much.

"Why not now?" he asked.

"No money," she said honestly. "It's just Grams and me, and she just gets a little money from social security, and then whatever I make cleaning, and I help Grams with bills when I can. Thankfully I got a scholarship for school, otherwise, I wouldn't have been able to do that either. In fact, I'm supposed to be in class right now." She said the last part while looking at him pointedly.

"Mmm." He hummed but didn't look guilty in the slightest. "What are you going to school for?" he asked instead.

"Human services," she said, perking up a little. She always liked talking about the kind of things she wanted to do in the future, even if she didn't know exactly how she was going to do it. "Chicago has a large homeless and underserved population, so I wanted to do something to help. I still haven't decided exactly how I'm going to do that, but I figured a degree was a good place to start. There are lots of cities and people around the world who get lost in the cracks of the system, and helping makes me feel like I'm *doing* something and not wasting my life. You know?"

Zaid looked lost in thought. "Rhapta could probably use something like that," he said with a curl of his lip.

"Really? Are there a lot of poor or homeless?" she asked, curious.

He nodded just as their food arrived. A huge plate of fried fish and vegetables and a side of fries for her, Zaid only got a small bowl of fruit. She didn't comment on his lack of necessary food groups and instead started devouring her own plate.

"Over the last fifty years or so, the population has been dwindling to the point where the city is half empty and a quarter of the people who are left live in the slums."

"Why?" she asked around a mouthful of fries.

"A few reasons," he said, taking a deep breath. "Ubir have always been a problem. Some Anunnaki just don't want to be confined to the city and don't want to relinquish their abilities. But we've never had as many as we do now. A few of the Elders think it is due to the deteriorating psychic barrier around the city."

At her confused expression, he elaborated. "There is a barrier of psychic energy that permeates the city. It's what allows us to speak telepathically to each other, keep the city invisible and protected, helps the food grow. For the most part, it comes from the Aurastones, but it's supposed to include the people's energy as well, so both energies work in tandem. As people leave the city, there is less energy from them to hold the barrier. With the collapsing barrier, it makes life less appealing to live there. Abilities weaken, food spoils, people become worried that we won't be able to hide the city eventually either. So they leave.

"There are pockets just outside the city itself that still benefit from the protection but don't receive any of the bene-fits. These are the slums where the poor go and those who don't agree with the Elders and want to leave but won't commit to it. The Rhaptan government tries to help them, but it's clear they care less for those who don't want to participate in upholding the barrier. So that, mixed with the ubir makes a big problem that is getting harder to fix."

"That sounds... bad," she said truthfully. She had finished almost everything on her plate except for a stray pickle that was mixed in with the vegetables. "Is there no way to fix it?"

He shrugged. "Not that I know of, other than having enough people come back into the city to boost the psychic energy. What's even worse is there are a few underground rebel groups that have started to form. They are people who truly despise the Elder's rule and want a democracy. Other groups want a monarchy back. Are you going to eat that?" he asked, pointing at her pickle.

"What?" Apparently, that was answer enough as he picked it off her plate and popped it into his mouth.

"What?" he answered back. "Pickles are one of the few human foods I actually enjoy. I'm not going to let you waste it."

Kinza just stared at him a moment. "Uh, no, it's fine. I don't like pickles. You said monarchy?"

"Yeah, up until a few hundred years ago, Rhapta was ruled by a line of kings. When the last king died, his heir went missing the same night, and the line ended."

"Why don't you just pick a new king?"

"There is a bit of a debate about that." He poked at the remains of his fruit. "Most scholars think it was because that particular line was more attuned with Aurastone and had a stronger psychic presence. Some people believe only that line was chosen by the heavens to guide us, and no one else will do." He shrugged. "It doesn't really make a difference now. I just do my job and get paid, and that's that."

"Hmph," she said, crossing her arms. He almost seemed as if he didn't care much about his people. But how could you not? A whole race of people was dying out, and there didn't look to be anyone *doing* anything about it. Before she got a chance to question him more, he stood up.

"All right, let's get going. We still need to steal a car before we leave."

Kinza rolled her eyes. "Of course we do."

CHAPTER 16

INTO THE DARKNESS OF THE MOUNTAIN

The wind whipped through the open windows of the car, rippling Zaid's shirt in a way that wasn't unpleasant.

They had found a car parked in an alley a few minutes' walk from where they were. It was an old silver thing with the windows already down and the keys under the visor. They had gotten lucky. A few minutes later, he was winding through the evening traffic. It was later than he had thought it had been, and the sun was on its downward arc. They still had a few hours of daylight, though.

Kinza turned the radio onto some local reggae station and propped her feet up on the dash. She looked peaceful for the moment, and he didn't want to bother her. Soon after they had sat down to eat, he had felt a familiar sensation of another Aura moving near him. Similar to large sea creatures passing each other in the deep waters. They weren't seen but could be felt by the waves they caused. Being so close to Rhapta, it wasn't unlikely for it to be another *venari* passing through, but at the lack of contact the other Aura presented, he was doubtful. He had kept his eye out for any dark figures and his mind out for any encroaching Auras. It wasn't worthwhile to listen for heartbeats as they were everywhere here.

Thankfully no cars tailed them as they left the busier parts of the town. They entered onto the main highway heading east for ten minutes before getting back off, taking a side road north. It was a popular route for those looking to hike the mountain, but they would be getting off this road long before that. He had taken this way so many times over the years he could do it in his sleep.

"Are you going to stay for my trial?" Kinza asked over the roar of the wind and the radio station. He turned it down so he didn't have to yell. Human music always sounded so chaotic and noisy.

"I was going to take you to Tahir first, and then they would take you to the trial from there. *Venari* have no reason to be at the trials; we just bring people in." He didn't mention he hadn't watched an ubir trial in seven years. He had never had the stomach for them after the last one he had witnessed. Kinza frowned at his response, and he rethought his plans. "Do you want me to?"

She looked back out the window and nodded, and said "yes" almost too quiet for him to hear. Her ponytail whipped around her collar in the wind. Zaid gripped the steering wheel a little tighter. If she wanted him to go with her, then he would make himself stomach it for one day. They would most likely figure out what was going on before that. It was possible she wouldn't even need a trial, depending on what the Elders said.

They were silent for the next half hour, watching the buildings eventually give way to more trees as they got closer to the jungle surrounding the mountain. A few cars traveled this way with them, and Zaid was ever-aware of which ones stayed on this route. Eventually they got deep into the jungle and just before a sharp bend in the road he put the hazard lights on and pulled over onto the side of the road.

"What are we doing?" Kinza asked as two cars maneuvered around them and continued on. Zaid pulled a little further off the road and into the trees.

"This is where we stop. We walk from here." He got out and started pulling vines and branches over the car. It really wasn't that big of a deal to leave it here, it was unlikely someone would actually look into it, but he did it just in case.

Kinza got out and stretched. Several joints popped in protest. The fading light of day skimmed across the treetops to land on her face. For a moment, she verily glowed in the sunlight, and he had a hard time looking away.

He remembered the Aura in Moshi and focused again on his surroundings. They were at the edge of the jungle, and he was just now realizing how dark it was. His original plan was to just pick her up, and he could make the trip to the barrier in ten minutes. But it now looked too dark between the trees for him to move that fast. He sighed; they would have to walk.

"Let's get going," he said. "We are running out of daylight." He didn't look but could hear her heartbeat as she followed behind him. The sounds of birds chirping echoed around them as they stepped fully between the trees. Every few feet, he heard Kinza trip behind him, occasionally swearing at the unmoving foliage. *This is going to take forever.*

"Do you have any family? Or a girlfriend or a wife or something?" she asked after about twenty minutes of her tripping.

He thought for a moment of Amir and wondered what he would have thought of her. He decided he would have liked her and then promptly buried the feeling down into that dark place. "My mother lives in Rhapta." After a moment, he said, "You'd like her."

Why did I say that?

"And no, I do not have a girlfriend or a wife or something. I told you, *venari* don't have time for things like that."

"So you aren't allowed to live your life at all? Just this until you die?" A root snapped under her foot, and she stumbled to the side before righting herself.

"Yes."

"Why would you choose to do that? I would just quit and do something else."

"I didn't get to choose. I was chosen to do this. All *venari* are."

"Wait, what? Really?" She tried to jog closer but just managed to run into a swath of foliage trapping in her hair. He sighed and turned to help her, gently removing the leaves and twigs from her dark strands.

"Yes, some people get to choose what kind of job they want, others are chosen for their abilities. People with combative abilities are chosen to be warriors. Stealth and sight abilities are typically chosen for the scouts surrounding the city. Healing abilities are chosen to be healers. You get the idea." He turned and kept walking, trying not to get distracted by her nearness. His steps moved a little quicker.

"Ah, so running super-fast and hearing heartbeats is good for a hunter. Do the people with mediocre abilities get to choose what they want to do?"

"Sometimes, yes, it just depends on what we are running short on."

"What does your mom do?"

He smiled, thinking of his mother sitting in their home, covered in piles of silks she was mending. "She's a seamstress. Her ability is sight." He chuckled. "She can see like a hawk, so if you're within range, there's no hiding from her."

Kinza groaned. "My mom used to be like that, except with hearing. I swear, I could be up in my room, quiet as a mouse, and at the first crinkle of a candy bar, you could hear my name from down the street."

Zaid laughed at the image of a younger Kinza hiding with sweets in her room. "How—" He paused, regretting asking, but Kinza caught on.

"They were murdered," she said quietly. "I came home from the park one day, and Grams had just found them in the living room. They never found who did it. Not a shred of evidence." She said it as if it was just old history now.

He stopped to look at her. Losing his father had only been hard on his mother as she was the only one who remembered him. But after Amir, he couldn't fathom losing his mother as well. And here Kinza was, going to school to make the world a better place. Giving her money to her grandmother and smiling while she did it. There just weren't people like that. He had been all over the world, and people were greedy and self-ish. It was almost an oddity to find someone who put others before themselves and did so willingly. But, he supposed, Kinza was an oddity in more ways than one.

"I'm sorry," he said simply. "I know what it is like to lose family." He turned back before he said something stupid.

They walked along for another thirty minutes, but the light was almost non-existent. Kinza kept tripping over every other root, and even he could hardly see in front of himself. "All right, we are going to need to stop for the night."

"Here?" she asked, looking around them. They stood next to a tall tree, as wide around as a small car, large roots extending in every direction. It was as good of shelter as they were going to get.

"Yes, this looks good. We'll leave as soon as it's light out again. Stay here a moment. I'll build a fire."

He left her standing by the tree and within minutes had a good selection of logs and sticks. After a few fruitless attempts at starting a fire by hand—and a few ill-timed snickers from Kinza—he pulled a lighter out of his duffel bag, and the little pile of logs was roaring within moments.

"Won't someone see this?" she asked, sitting down by the ring of logs. Unfortunately, he needed to sit with his back to the tree to keep an eye out, so it forced him to sit just a few feet from her. She didn't seem to notice, though.

He shook his head. "No, no one really goes this way. We are getting close enough to the city that humans tend to avoid this area, even if they don't know why."

She just nodded. "I've never gone camping before," she said, looking around into the trees. "I supposed I've never left the country before either."

Zaid thought for a moment, considering how Anunnaki were confined to one city, but he had seen the world. On the flip side, humans had the world, and she had only seen a tiny corner of it. "I'm glad we could cross so many firsts off for you in one day. Anything else you think we can squeeze in tonight?"

Kinza's mouth popped open, and he immediately realized his mistake. "I didn't mean—" he said at the same time as she said, "No, of course—"

"Wait, I really didn't mean anything by that," he tried to say, but it came out in a garbled mess.

"No... I, uh, no, I totally get it. No worries."

"Sorry," he muttered pathetically. He had heard her heart rate pick up, and now he mentally groaned and wanted to hurl himself off the nearest cliff. Embarrassing her was the last thing he wanted to do.

They sat in awkward silence for several minutes before she spoke. "What happens after my trial?"

He looked over at her, the firelight illuminating half her face. She pulled her knees up to her chest.

"Say they agree that I'm not ubir and that my abilities are just a fluke or something. Do they just send me home, and that's the end of it?"

"Hmm, they would most likely want to make sure you have a good measure of control over your abilities first, but this hasn't ever happened before. That being said, I don't see why they wouldn't just let you go. The only reason they don't let the rest of us wander around is that we essentially become human, or some choose to become ubir. There really isn't a third option for us."

"Would you take me home then?"

He hadn't considered the *after* part, and now it was starting to sour his mood. "They will probably send me on another mission before I get the chance. They would most likely drop you off back at Moshi and tell you to figure it out from there."

"So... I probably won't see you after I go in for my trial then." Her matter-of-fact tone rang an odd sort of bell for him. She was staring intently into the fire now, as if something she saw in its depths confused her.

"Yes... I suppose," he said slowly. He flicked a twig into the fire and watched it burn.

"Hmm, and what if I wanted to be *venari*? Would they let me do that?"

"*What*?!" he snapped, whipping his head in her direction. Had she really said that? The entire idea was entirely ridiculous. "Why would you want that? *No one* wants that."

"Well..." She took a deep breath. "Then I could go all around the world and see lots of places like you do. And catching ubir seems like a good thing for the world. And you can teach whatever I need to know."

Totally preposterous. The thought that someone *wanted* to do this was confusing him on another level. "You would— you would want... to come with me?" She turned to look at him fully then. Her eyes were dark enough that he felt he was staring into the night sky, and she leaned slightly toward him.

"Yes."

KINZA DIDN'T KNOW what she was saying, but she realized she meant it.

The thought of just going home after her trial like nothing ever happened seemed almost abhorrent. If even she was able to control her abilities, how was she supposed to live the rest of her life knowing that these people exist and she is apart from them? And the thought of leaving without Zaid nearly confused her.

She didn't know how she felt about him anymore. At first, she hated him for taking her, then she disliked him for how cold he seemed, and now... now she didn't know what she felt. He clearly was trying to take care of her the best he could, even if it was in his own way. Somehow, within three days, he had managed to carve out a portion of her mind and decided to camp out there. *Not* having him around to argue with felt... odd.

But being able to do what he did, traveling the world, ridding it of dangerous people? Now that she felt sure about. She could learn and help and travel all at the same time. It was something she never imagined would be a possibility for her. The thought made her excited.

"Yes," she said again. "I want to do what you do." She smiled and looked back into the fire. The ease in which she had just made that decision didn't even bother her. It just felt *right*.

"Kinza," he said patiently. "No one wants to be *venari* for a reason. We are basically shunned by the Anunnaki, but we don't fit within human societies either. We are always alone."

She wrinkled her nose. "Why would you be shunned? You are doing so much good for the world."

He shook his head and leaned back against the tree. "*Venari* are shunned because what we do is considered dirty work. We clean up the filth of our people while spending much of our lives in human society, which is still considered 'other' to Anunnaki. Rhapta may exist to guide humanity, but that doesn't mean we want to exemplify it. *Venari* are a reminder of humans."

Kinza scoffed. "You said that before, that Anunnaki guide humans. It sounds more like you avoid us at all costs."

"We don't have the option to live outside of the city as we are. And when we are sent out, it's to run errands for the Elders. It happens rarely, but sometimes we need to interfere with humanity to keep them from killing themselves. We sway business deals, influence markets, help future leaders, and less commonly, assassinate those who would cause widespread destruction in the future."

Kinza's excitement was turning to curdled milk in her stomach. She knew Anunnaki had an impact on humanity, but this was more extensive than what she had imagined. And Zaid acted like it was common knowledge, as if it didn't even matter. "That feels controlling to me. The Elders sound like they like the control they have over the city and over humanity and are happy to hide in their little city, so they don't have to interact with the dirty humans." Killing ubir was one thing, but assassinating innocent humans before they even did anything to justify the action? The thought disgusted her.

Zaid threw his hands up and didn't respond.

His lack of answer only made her angry. "It's almost barbaric. You treat us like animals, herding us around like sheep and slaughtering the ones who don't look right. Is that why there are assassins after me? Am I a *threat*?" She laughed, but there was no humor in it. "It sounds like Anunnaki dying out is evolution's way of saying they are trash."

Zaid just shrugged, going quiet again. "Yeah, maybe."

She whirled on him. "I don't understand you. One minute you are telling me to respect your people, and the next, you couldn't care less if they died out. I'm a little confused here, so help a girl out. Do you actually care about anything or not?"

"Shut up, Kinza." It only made her boil with anger.

"Oh, don't worry. I know what your problem is." She couldn't stop now. The bitterness was choking her. "Haris told me all about your little sob story and how you had to execute your own brother. Maybe you finally realized how sick and twisted Anunnaki are, and you actually enjoyed it!" She spat the words at him.

Zaid froze, still as ice. He looked at her for a moment, and fear spiked through her at the look of death in his eyes. A moment later, he was gone, moving faster than she could follow.

She sat there for several minutes, inhaling through her nose and back out her mouth. After too many breaths to count, the anger cooled, and she realized she had gone too far—way too far.

She pounded a fist against her forehead, and tears pricked her eyes. The Anunnaki's treatment of humans and their own *venari* had disgusted her, but she hadn't meant to take it out on him. In fact, she had been angry *for* him somewhere at the beginning of the conversation.

He was right. She wasn't able to control her own emotions. She was lucky she hadn't been afraid, otherwise, she could have killed him by accident. How had she become so destructive?

There was only darkness and the sounds of the forest beyond the ring of firelight. It was lonely, and she deserved it. With nothing else to do and no way to apologize, she curled up into a ball on the ground and tried to sleep, tears slipping through the cracks in her eyelids.

Zaid ran for fifteen minutes before he decided to turn back. He wanted to be angry, but he just felt gutted. There were too many emotions, more than he had had in years, and it took time to bury them. She had all but said she wanted to stay with him in one breath and the next claimed his people deserved to die. Did she truly mean that?

He had seen the fear and anger in her eyes when he had mentioned the assassins. It was something he honestly hadn't thought of before. Could the Elders have sent someone to kill her? Was she prophesied to cause mass destruction to humanity? The thought of walking her into the arms of an assassin at Rhapta's gate made his chest hurt. She didn't deserve that.

Remembering the assassins had him moving a bit quicker.

Suddenly, he felt two Auras come out of nowhere and coming closer. He stopped to listen, but they were moving rapidly.

Dammit.

He took off in Kinza's direction again. He shouldn't have left her by herself, regardless of how she made him feel. The Auras were almost on top of him now, but he couldn't see anyone. He listened and heard one set of near-silent footsteps coming through the trees, but only shadows twisted in that direction. He spun around, listening for the other set of footsteps but heard nothing.

Something moved between the trees. Zaid pulled out his dagger. A third and then a fourth Aura came into his senses.

This was bad. Really bad.

Zaid clamped his hands over his ears as the high-pitched ring of a Deathstone appeared. His skull felt like it was splitting, and he gasped for breath and tried to fight it. More Deathstones were pulled out as a set of feet entered the small clearing he was in.

Zaid fell to his knees. Just before he passed out, he saw a pair of sickly green eyes looking at him from within the darkness.

CHAPTER 17

UNFATHOMABLE REALITIES

SEVEN YEARS EARLIER

Zaid made his way down the spiral staircase that led deep into the earth. Like most of Rhapta, it was made of limestone, but the way was dark. He carried a torch with him to light the way, he had learned the first time that one could easily fall down a flight of stairs in the dark, and no one would come to help you.

He had come this way a hundred times before in training but never had he descended into the cells of the city to see one of his own captives. Especially not his brother.

It had been two weeks since he had brought Amir back. After capturing him in Osaka he had brought him to the portal which opened up in a small town south of Mount Kilimanjaro, and from there, they had walked to the city's edge and entered. It had been one of the hardest times of his life to learn how far gone his brother really was.

Amir could barely walk, stumbling along like a madman. He would laugh hysterically and then lash out like a rabid dog a moment later. Zaid had broken down and tried pleading with him several times, but it never made any difference. Amir would continue on mumbling about blood and kings and flesh and prophecies.

There had been one moment when they had stopped on the side of the road, on the way to Rhapta, for a rest. Amir had turned to him and, with eyes completely focused, and all traces of madness gone, had said, *You got tall, little brother.*

Zaid had stared at him, believing he had been dreaming. But a minute later, Amir had fallen back into madness and tried to eat a lizard he had found on the ground. He didn't make it to his mouth before Zaid had caught him, but he still managed to rip the poor animal to shreds in his bound hands. He laughed and rolled in the yellow grass.

It was because of that moment that Zaid descended into the earth again. He wanted to see his brother one more time before the trial, just to see if there was a spark of the person he knew still in there. If there was, maybe he could petition on his behalf. Maybe he could beg a healer again to try and fix him.

Zaid knew the very real possibility that Amir would not be found redeemable in his trial, and the thought scared him to his core. If that happened, he had already planned to hide in the outskirts of the city, maybe at Khalil's, for a week. He didn't want to be inside of the city, inside of the collective Aura when his brother's life was taken. He couldn't bear it.

After he had brought Amir in, he was only allowed one day's reprieve before he was sent on another mission. He went home to his mother and told her he had found his brother. She had shouted and screamed at him, telling him to never lie to her. Eventually, she had fallen to the floor, her gut-wrenching sobs could be heard out in the courtyard and down the street. Everyone knew then what had happened.

Zaid had held her as she clung to him. A few hours later,

she had cried herself to sleep, and he tucked her into bed. He didn't dare leave without seeing her in the morning, so he slept there that night. She was already up when he woke, puffy-eyed but no longer crying. She kissed him goodbye, and he said he would be back soon.

He hated to leave her, but he had no choice. The *venari* were strict and would come knocking if he didn't appear before his next mission. After he had completed his initial year of training, Savar had come to him again and placed his Aurastone on Zaid's chest. He knew what to expect this time, and the stone became hot only for a moment. When he looked down again, it had grown to twine across his chest and up to the bottom of his neck.

Congratulations, Savar had said. *You are a venari now.* Zaid had felt nothing.

Before every mission, he would go to Savar, who would do the same thing. The tattoo would fade within a month if he didn't keep up with it, and then he wouldn't be able to go into the world without his Aura fading.

He had completed another mission, this one in Chile, with ease. It was so simple this time, and he was back within a few days. He completed two more before he returned for his brother's trial. He would be allowed a few days to attend. The trial itself would be just one day, though.

Zaid finally reached the bottom of the stairs and nodded to the guard who stood at the bottom. The guard nodded back in respect. Most people in the city shied away from him entirely now, but the guards stationed in the cells always seemed less afraid. Maybe because they saw what the *venari* truly did for Rhapta. Going out into the strange world and capturing people who were almost monsters. It was the one place in the city where he was treated like that. It was funny. He had to be in an underground dungeon with rows upon rows of people swimming in madness before he would receive an ounce of respect.

Zaid walked to the end of the long hall, passing rows of limestone cells set with obsidian bars. The cells themselves looked plain, but he knew that the stone around each one was embedded with *laqueus* so that all abilities were dampened. Depending on the ubir's particular ability, some were bound with it as well.

He took a right and walked halfway down this hall as well, stopping before a cell on the left. The few around it were empty. There were more cells down here than they would ever need. Hopefully.

Inside sat Amir. He was not bound with *laqueus,* but he was chained to the wall. His head was slumped to his chest. Zaid unlocked the bars and stepped inside. All *venari* had a key to the cells just in case. They were the ones who put them there, after all.

As the door rattled shut, Amir lifted his head. His eyes focused and unfocused as he squinted at Zaid's face. He looked drunk and feverish. His hair had grown much longer, and he smelled like a rotting corpse.

Little brother, Amir said, giving him a lopsided smile. Zaid looked down and caught sight of his tattoo on his left side. The last time he had seen it, he had been slightly jealous of how normal it looked. He had wanted his own to look like that. But instead, the once-beautiful mandala extended across his abdomen and to his back. Instead of sleek dark ink, it was raised and red, almost as if it was infected. It looked painful.

Hello, Amir, do you know why I am here?

Amir jerked at the chains a little. *Come, you are not supposed to be here... you are too young,* he mumbled, head lolling back and forth.

What?

Amir let out a high-pitched giggle, spit foaming out of his mouth. *There is blood smeared over the light. Did you know that? I couldn't find the passage, but the blood got in the way of the pages.*

I don't know what you are talking about. I came here so you could talk to me, so you could convince me you are still you. You do know who I am, right?

Amir looked at him again with unfocused eyes and held steady. Zaid waited with bated breath and hoped the brother he knew would surface.

Amir launched forward with a scream, teeth aimed at Zaid's face, only the chains holding him back. He growled and screamed like a wild animal. The hope that had risen in Zaid's chest had melted away, and a burning, dry ache remained.

His brother laughed at his face, rising in pitch. Zaid left the cell and locked it. Walking down the hall and back up to the staircase, he could hear his brother's maniacal laughter the entire way.

THE LIGHT STREAMING in from the skylights landed right upon the Grand Elder's chair in the largest council room of the Grand Hall. Zaid assumed that it had been strategic but still marveled at its placement.

The council room was rectangular like the rest of the building. At the far wall, a semicircular formation of fifty chairs were placed, looking a bit more like thrones, with the Grand Elder's chair in the middle. Grand Elder Hakim was truthfully there only for official propriety, as his mind was almost always addled with prophecy, some relevant and others not.

Before the Elders, a short-chain was nailed into the marble floor. That was where Amir would go. A crowd of people stood on both sides of the long aisle leading up to the chain, and the only light came from a few sconces on the wall and the skylights up above.

Zaid waited to one side of the aisle as was his duty. He stood with Savar and a few other *venari*, all of them older than him. Next to them were a few other administrative members of various councils governing the city. Across the aisle was where citizens were allowed to stand and watch. Anyone could attend the trials, and it was occasionally encouraged so as people could see the consequences of defecting to become an ubir.

His mother stood among a few friends of hers. She held her head high, but even from where he stood, he could see the deep hollows under her eyes and the sharpness of her cheekbones. He mentally reminded himself to make sure she was eating. Anunnaki didn't need much, but they did have to eat eventually.

The doors at the opposite end of the room opened, and a long stream of Elders made their way in, followed by a few guards. It took quite a while to get them all settled as they were all old and moved slowly. Once they were all in place, an attendant whispered in Grand Elder Hakim's ear, and he thumped a staff on the floor.

Bring in the prisoner.

Through the same doors walked Amir. His hands were chained behind his back, and four guards walked on all sides of him. He lurched and stumbled as he stepped, and his breaths came in and out as a wheeze. They chained him to the spot on the floor before the Elders. Hakim thumped his staff again at the whispering of his attendant.

Let the trial begin.

Over the next hour, several Elders, attendants, and a healer all attempted to question Amir. They asked him about his life prior to defecting, who he had talked with, the rebel groups he might have come in contact with, and his family. They only got snippets of speech and mumbled words. Sometimes he would laugh at them, and other times he would snap his teeth and wrench at the chains.

Zaid had been solely locking the sadness he felt for his brother in a box. The anger he had felt in Osaka was still there but had dulled at Amir's momentary lucidity on their journey. Regardless, he knew the outcome of the trial and had mentally prepared for it the same as his mother had appeared to. That didn't stop her from screaming when the verdict came in.

The prisoner has been deemed too sick with the madness of blood magic. He will be put to death. Hakim thumped his staff once more to signify the end of the trial.

Zaid's mother had screamed, and a few other women held her as she cried. She quieted down quickly after the initial verdict, but tears still fell on the marble floor. Amir would be taken back to his cell, and one of the older *venari* would complete his execution at dawn. The *venari* that were too old to work in the field were resigned to that task.

As the Elders moved to stand, one of them spoke.

Elder Yuvaan cleared his throat, and the others turned to look at him. He was the representative of the warriors and frequently had strong opinions about the rest of the council. *Excuse me, Elders. I want to raise a query.* He turned to Elder Ishar. *Ishar, is it not true that every venari must execute his first convicted ubir himself?*

All thoughts drained from Zaid's head.

The Elders spoke in whispers, and the people at the side turned to each other. What rule was this? None of them remembered it.

Ishar closed his eyes as if it pained him to say the next words. *Technically, Yuvaan, you are correct. That was a law enacted centuries ago, but it has since fallen out of practice.*

Fallen out of practice? Then it was not removed? Yuvaan asked.

What difference does it make, Yuvaan? Elder Tahir asked. *The deed will be completed as always.*

Zaid couldn't think. He couldn't breathe.

Ishar sighed but nodded grimly. *Yes, Yuvaan is correct.* The other Elders began whispering furiously, and the crowd turned to look at Zaid.

Yuvaan spoke again. *Then I think if it is a rule, we should adhere to it. Or do none of our rules matter now?* The chattering became louder, and the inside of Zaid's head became quieter. After several minutes of deliberation, Hakim banged his staff for silence.

We have decided to uphold this law. At sunrise tomorrow, Amir Hatem's execution will commence at the hands of the venari who brought him in.

From somewhere in the back of his shattering mind, Zaid heard his mother scream.

THE SUN'S rays peeked over Rhapta, setting the tops of the buildings a delicate gold.

Zaid walked down the main boulevard as he had been all night. He had not slept once. The decision had come from the Elders, and everything afterward was a blur. He had felt far away from his body, as if he was looking down, watching himself move around in the world. From up high, he had seen his mother scream and frantically beg the Elders for mercy. She said she had lost her husband, her firstborn, and she did not want to lose the mind of her youngest.

They dismissed her.

He watched as his body walked right by the crowd of

people, not seeing them whisper and stare at him. If they had moved away from him before, they avoided him like the plague now. His body walked down the hall, past the statues at the center of the Grand Hall, through the north wing and out onto the Grand Plaza. The sun had been setting, and he started walking.

Through the northern quarter, his body walked past the warrior's training grounds, to the east where his mother's house was, and to the south where the quarries lay, and finally to the west to the abandoned building he had run to years before.

He looked at the tiny lavender flowers that grew on the vines and reminded him of his mother, and he looked at the spot he had fallen asleep, only to find Amir there later coaxing him back home.

Zaid watched as he turned and left. He walked through the streets all night even as the air cooled and his body longed for warmth. *He* couldn't feel it, though. He was too high up, too removed to feel the cold.

As the hours went by, he settled back into his body, but he didn't stop there. He collected every emotion that threatened to end him, bound them all up tight, and buried them down. Down so far, it was as if he was placing them in the earth's mantle, and then he filled that dark place back up. Covered it so the emotions couldn't get back out and hurt him. He knew if they came back, he would die. He would shatter into a hundred thousand pieces.

He made his way slowly to the cells in the center of the city. Without the emotions, there was a cooling mist settled at the edge of his mind. It was a gentle balm, just like...

His mind shut the thought out.

The door to the cells came quicker than he expected. Elder Ishar was there to make sure he showed up, and Elder Tahir was there. He placed a heavy hand on Zaid's shoulder in compassion. Savar was there as well, and handed him a long, wicked-looking obsidian dagger and nodded to Zaid, face grim.

Zaid had found through the last several years that Savar was immensely strict and his training was harsh, but he wasn't cold-hearted, and his punishments were just. He didn't agree with the Elder's decision in this, but he would obey.

He entered the door and descended the long staircase into the bowels of the earth. The end came too soon, and the guard at the door looked at him, not even nodding today. Zaid walked as if in a dream, the last stretch to his brother's cell. The whole way, he mentally put up a shield of obsidian and bone and ice in his mind to ward out the emotions, just in case.

The cell was before him, and Amir sat in the same spot as before. He laughed and twisted as Zaid entered.

Zaid felt hollow, like his arms and legs held nothing inside of them as he entered and drew the blade. But he wouldn't wait. He wouldn't hesitate.

Amir's head rolled in his direction, and he looked with unfocused eyes. He smiled.

Hello, little br—

A line of blood spread quickly over Amir's throat and dripped down his chest. Zaid turned and left the cell. Walking back through the halls, up the spiral staircase, and into the morning light.

CHAPTER 18

BLOOD AS DARK AS RUBIES

Kinza moved through a dead city. Crumbled walls looked as if they had been abandoned centuries ago, and the forest started to grow within the cracks, pushing stone apart. A weak sun filtered through the heavy mist, lighting her way just enough as she stumbled through the streets. There was no one here. Not a single living soul. But shadows twisted at the edges of her vision, trailing her as she walked.

She needed to get to the center of the city, but she couldn't remember why. There was something she had to do, but what? She walked for a while, and the shadows followed her, coming ever closer. Faint sounds came from their direction that resembled something like speech. It was harsh and clipped, and she couldn't understand, but an overwhelming sense of danger started creeping over her skin.

Now running, she flew through the streets, avoiding dark corners and shooting away from the whispering shadows until she came upon a large plaza. She saw a statue that looked vaguely familiar but didn't stop until she got the massive azure stone in the middle. It was humming an insistent song, and she needed to get *closer. The shadows were in the plaza now, moving through the mist like fish in a stream.*

They were going to kill her. She felt it in their voices, even if she didn't understand the words. They reeked of malevolence, but Kinza couldn't worry about that now. The stone was all that mattered. She just couldn't remember why. Her eyes closed, and without thinking, she placed her hand upon it.

It was as cold as ice.

Her eyes flew open, and she was standing in a vast hall lined with statues. At first, she thought nothing was there, but then she turned and noticed the body on the floor. Coming close to it, she saw a pool of blood carrying its life essence away. It was lying face down, so she turned it over.

It was Zaid—and he was dead.

No, no, no, no, no, *her mind begged. She grabbed his shoulder and shook him. This was all her fault. She did this but couldn't remember how. She just did. Tears splashed down on the stiff body as she realized her efforts were hopeless.*

At the edges of the room, the mist crept in, bringing muttering shadows with it. They had found her, and there was nowhere to run. They were closing in, and there was nothing she could do.

She gasped as a hand clamped down on her wrist. Looking down, she watched as Zaid's eyes flew open, and he spoke.

Kinza.

Kinza gasped awake and looked around. The fire had dwindled to embers, but the forest was still dark. Sitting up, she tried to breathe slowly, sweat stuck her shirt and pants to her skin, and her heart galloped at invisible fears.

"Zaid?" she whispered into the darkness. She looked

around and saw that she was alone. It took her a moment to remember what had happened.

Their argument. The things she had said. Guilt washed over her again at the memory, and realized Zaid must not have come back. It had to have been at least a few hours though, would he not come back at all? Kinza started to panic, thinking he abandoned her in the forest, but she also felt it wouldn't be entirely unjustified.

What was she supposed to do? Maybe this was his way of saying she could go home. He knew she wasn't ubir; therefore, she wasn't his concern anymore and could leave. But would he really just leave her like this? She rocketed back and forth between the guilt of their conversation and the fear of being left out here.

The fire was nearly out, and she was getting cold. There was nothing left to do except walk then. She got up and picked a long, heavy stick that burned faintly at one end. It was the best she could do for some light. Slinging her backpack on, she tried to pick the direction they had come from and started walking.

She had only slept for a few hours at most and was still exhausted. There was little comfort in the embers on her stick, and she desperately missed Grams at the moment. Tears filled her eyes as she walked, making it even harder to see. She tripped several times but inhaled and kept going. It had to get lighter out eventually, and she would find the road, right?

The light from the stick only illuminated the smallest space in front of her, but it made the darkness between the trees twist and warp. Trying not to panic at her situation, she took longer, deeper breaths. The back of her neck started to tingle.

Kinza.

Her head snapped up. "Zaid?" she asked, looking around. There were only the trees and the vines and sounds of the forest. She kept walking and swore some of the shadows moved with her. The tingling traveled down her spine to her arms and legs, moving quickly.

Kinza. She heard it again. It was definitely Zaid's voice, faint, but his. "Zaid!" she called a bit louder this time. Walking faster wouldn't help as she just kept tripping, so she tried to keep her eyes trained in front of her, but her fearful heart wanted her to keep looking behind. She kept going for a few more minutes when it came again.

Kinza, run! She stopped and listened. Zaid's voice was coming from seemingly nowhere, and she didn't know which direction to walk. She also could have sworn she saw something move just a few feet from her. Her fears tripled when a twig snapped a few moments later.

Kinza ran. It was probably the worst thing she could have done because she immediately dropped her stick and tripped over a root, only to faceplant in the dirt. She heard footsteps and thought she would lose it from the fear alone, but the next second, a high-pitched, shrieking sound threatened to rip her eardrums out. Her bones rattled in her body as nausea came in waves. She groaned and clamped her hands over her ears, trying to hold her body together.

The sound only got louder, though, and within seconds she succumbed to the sweet darkness of oblivion.

THE SMELL of fire woke Kinza this time. Thankfully, no nightmares plagued her sleep. Instead, she woke to a living one.

Cracking her eyes open, she looked around. The sound of water drew her gaze to a small river about twenty feet in front of her. She was in a clearing close to the edge, surrounded by three fires in a semi-circle around her. The source of her fears stood at the water's edge; two people stood wrapped in night-dark cloth from head to toe. The only thing exposed was one of their faces. It looked to be a man with deep brown eyes that sneered at the person he was arguing with. The other one looked slight enough to be a woman.

The assassins. Her breathing picked up but left her chest entirely when she looked to the right. Curled up against a tree was Zaid, bound at ankle and wrist with a silvery-gray rope that she recognized as *laqueus*. His eyes were closed, and she couldn't tell if he was breathing. If she thought he had looked bad at the resort, this blew that thought out of the park.

Blood coated his face and chest. She could just make out uncountable lacerations covering his chest in the firelight. His face was slack, and she couldn't see if his chest was rising and falling from where she was lying.

She moved to get up, but a heavy boot shoved her back to the ground.

"Ah, awake are we?" the man by the river said, looking toward her. He spoke in broken English, and his voice was raspy, almost as if from disuse. "I wouldn't bother trying to stand, Yusuf there has been waiting for this." He nodded toward the person above her. She twisted, trying to get a look, and almost gasped.

It was the man that followed her home earlier that week. Even under the swathes of dark cloth, he was unmistakable. Just then, two more assassins appeared around the tree Zaid was against. She recognized the one with the sickly green eyes, and the other one made no sound as he walked.

"Rafiq has had a hard time tracking you," the man by the river one said, nodding toward the one with the green eyes. "And I don't think you've met Ghufran or Aisha here," he said, indicating the other man and the woman next to him. Why did it matter if she knew them? It was clear they wanted something from her, and then they were going to kill her. Regardless, the man walked closer and crouched down, a small smile on his face. He looked at her like a child looked at a puppy, like a toy for him to play with. "You may call me Jafar, Kinza. You've caused quite a load of problems, but we will sort this all out soon now, won't we?"

He stood and pulled out a long obsidian dagger, similar to the ones Zaid had.

"What the hell do you want?" Kinza snarled at him. "Why are you following me?"

The wicked point of the dagger glinted in the light as he went back and paced along the water's edge. "This is what we are going to do, my little Kinza. I need to ask you a few very specific questions, and I'm going to need you to answer them honestly. That's okay, isn't it?" he asked the last part mockingly.

When she didn't say anything, Jafar's eyes flicked to Yusuf behind her. Kinza grunted and a boot connected with her rib cage not once but three times. It shocked the breath out of her, and she gasped for air into the ground. "Good," Jafar said.

Kinza... she heard Zaid's voice again. Looking over, she saw his eyes were cracked open a slit, but it didn't look as if he had spoken. Ghufran saw where she was looking and crouched down before Zaid. He gripped his throat and lifted him up halfway off the ground.

"They're both awake, Jafar," Ghufran said in a similar raspiness, peering into Zaid's face before dropping him back to the ground.

Zaid struggled to sit up, and Kinza realized there were many more lacerations than she had originally thought, and his head was bobbing from the blood loss. She wanted to scream. No one deserved *this*. "Why did you hurt him? Aren't you both Anunnaki? On the same side?" she snapped at Jafar.

He had watched Zaid struggle with mild disinterest, and now that gaze swung to her. "There are no sides, little one. We are just doing what we have to, to protect our people. At the moment, he is in the way of that." He walked closer. "Now, let's hurry this up a bit. Your name is Kinza Solace, is it not?"

She scowled up at him. "That's a stupid question since you already knew that."

"I'm going to need you to be a bit more pleasant," Jafar said quietly. Out of the corner of her eye, she saw Rafiq poking at Zaid's chest, and he grunted in pain.

Kinza spat in Jafar's face.

Ever so slowly, he wiped it away and sighed. As fast as a viper, his hand shot out and gripped her arm. Pain exploded out of every nerve in her body, as bright and hot as if she had been on fire. She heard someone scream and realized it was herself. Her body spasmed as she tried to get away from Jafar's hand, but it was no use. He released her after an eternity, and she collapsed back onto the ground, sobbing.

Kinza! Zaid's voice shouted this time, and she thought it was in her head. She knew better than to look and just let herself lay in the dirt.

Zaid? she asked tentatively.

The woman by the water, Aisha, had started pacing, Jafar looking back toward her for a moment, clearly annoyed. Maybe they were talking in their minds as well.

Kinza, just hold on. You'll be fine, just hold on. It was Zaid! And he was talking in her head. She didn't care when or how it happened, but her sobs become ones of relief at his voice, even if they were both about to be dead.

"Your name is Kinza Solace, is it not?" Jafar asked again.

She just nodded this time.

"And your mother, her name was Sadia Solace, yes?"

At her mother's name, she went rigid. She hadn't heard anyone say her parents' names in years, and now this assassin from the other side of the planet was asking about her? She sat up as confusion racked her brain. How? How would he know her mother?

She had waited too long to respond, and he reached out to touch her again. "Yes!" she shouted. "That was her name. Why are you asking me about my mother?" she asked. She realized the tingling on her neck had not stopped this entire time and was still prickling over her arms and legs. At the mention of her mother, heat started to pool in her abdomen.

Jafar ignored her. "And did your mother have a tattoo?" he asked instead.

"Not that I remember," she tried to crawl backward, but Yusuf's boot connected with her back, throwing her forward. Jafar looked up in mild annoyance.

"But you do," Jafar said. He didn't phrase it as a question, but it was one. Looking to Yusuf again, they grabbed her arms and legs, pinning her to the ground on her back. Kinza truly started to panic, thrashing as hard as she could. It only lasted a moment, though, as Yusuf ripped her tank top up to reveal the tattoo on her abdomen.

It was glowing. Faintly, but in the darkness, it was unmistakable. She froze to look at it.

"There she is," Jafar whispered, more to himself than anyone. Ghufran's eyes snapped to where Aisha was standing. She must have said something to them in their minds.

"Jafar," Aisha said. It sounded like both a plea and a warning. He responded in a language she didn't recognize and stood up, releasing her. Yusuf had moved two steps back as well.

Zaid was fully awake now, struggling at his bonds; a few of them snapped. He didn't get more than a few inches before

Ghufran and Rafiq were punching and kicking him. He didn't stop, though, as they drew obsidian daggers.

"Stop!" Kinza screamed. "He didn't do anything, he was only doing his job. Just stop!" the last part came out in a sob. They ignored her, and new cuts appeared on Zaid's chest and arms. One of his eyes was nearly swollen shut now, and his breath came in labored gasps.

They must have received a silent order from Jafar because they both stepped back in unison, letting Zaid bleed out in the dirt. The firelight glinted against the blood that dripped to the ground. Kinza didn't know how good Anunnaki healing was, but she'd bet that they were trying to outpace it, so he was incapacitated.

"What do my tattoo and my mother have to do with anything?" she choked out. "We've never done anything to you."

Jafar had stepped back to survey her like a critic would consider a painting in a museum, one finger tapping at his chin. "It's not what you *have* done; it's what you *will* do." At her confused expression, he sighed and started pacing back and forth in small circles. He looked up at the night sky and said, "I suppose it doesn't hurt to tell you why. I'm not that cruel."

Kinza begged to differ. She had gotten to her knees, but Yusuf hovered closely behind her, an ever-threatening presence, so she didn't dare move further. Her eyes kept flicking back toward Zaid, who was now lying in the dirt, forcing his good eye open to look at her. He looked... guilty. It truly gutted her as she felt she was the one who should feel guilty. He had just wanted to do his job, and she was the wrench in the works.

"If you're not already aware of this," Jafar said. "There are many prophecies in the Anunnaki tribe. Some are for the near future, some predict the rain, others predict human wars, but only one has lasted almost two hundred years." He held up a finger. "It has been seen through visions of multiple Elders and non-Elders alike. Everyone knows it. Zaid here even knows it."

Zaid glared at Jafar with gritted teeth.

"What does that have to do with me?" Kinza asked warily.

"The prophecy goes that one day an Anunnaki born outside the tribe will return to the city. They will have abilities unknown and will bring down chaos and destruction upon the city, ending the lines of Anunnaki for good."

"That's not—" Zaid started to shout, but Rafiq's boot connected with his mouth. Aisha stood by the water, keeping one foot in and one out, but even beneath the folds of dark cloth, a certain tenseness held her body. Was she not in agreement with the others?

Jafar turned to glare at Zaid for a moment and then back to Kinza. "It's fairly simple, yes? Although those who have the visions speak of the gruesomeness of the foretelling. Rhapta would be nothing more than ash, and the people dead or vanished. A kind of hell would emerge in what we now call home."

Kinza snorted. "And you think I'm that person?"

"I do now, yes, but we had a sort of... hiccup last time?" he said.

"What do you—" She stopped. Ice flooded her veins and her vision narrowed as she started to understand.

"You see, we were told where to find you... just not *when* we would find you," he said.

No. Her heart started pounding, trying to escape her chest. She couldn't slow her breaths as she started to hyperventilate.

Kinza, Zaid said in her mind. *Kinza, breathe. Don't listen to him.*

"The thing is," Jafar said, looking a mockery of guilt, "we were told it would be a young woman by the name of Solace. And ten years ago, we found her pretty easily. There was the unfortunate business of the husband getting in the way as well, but it was considered a job well done."

Kinza's lungs stuttered as she started weeping. Half of her hair had come loose and now hung around her face, sticking to the tears. She wrapped her arms around her middle and held on, hoping she wouldn't fall apart right there in the dirt. There it was. She had lived without knowing what happened to them for ten years, and there was the answer, standing all around her.

Hadn't she wanted this? Hadn't she wanted to know? No, this was worse. So much worse, knowing her parents paid a price that was supposed to be hers.

"But several years went by," Jafar continued. She didn't know how there could be more to this. She wanted it to stop. "People still had the visions of the outsider when they should have stopped. Then not too long ago, our Grand Elder Hakim had another vision. This time he told us he saw something different. The outsider could be known by a mark, a tattoo just like our own. Except hers would be larger, but different from the *venari* or the ubir. And then you know the rest of the story," he said, waving in her direction.

Kinza still sobbed. She felt weak and powerless; there was nothing she could do. The knowledge couldn't save her parents now. They were long dead, bodies cold in the ground. And how could she blame the Anunnaki for coming after her? They were just trying to protect their people. She felt like she was turning into nothing, like dust floating away on the wind. Grams would be broken when she never came home. How would she ever know what happened? Her throat constricted as the familiar tingling and heat racked her body along with the tears. Everything *hurt*.

Aisha had started pacing again along the water's edge. Light was just starting to come over the treetops. It glinted on the river, and Kinza could see it moving lazily downstream. In contrast, Aisha's steps back and forth looked like rapids down the side of a mountain. Something was making her anxious, and Ghufran and Rafiq kept glancing in her direction, holding onto their knives.

Jafar came close and crouched down again, brushing a strand of hair out of Kinza's face. The brief contact sent a momentary shock of pain that was gone as soon as it came. "It's a shame, really," he said so quietly only she could hear. "You are such a pretty thing." His eyes roved over her face hungrily, but his reverie was broken by Zaid's thrashing behind him. He had gotten mostly loose from his bonds. He was shouting in the same language they had spoken before. Jafar sighed and said a bit louder, "We can deal with that first if it makes you feel a bit better." He stood and walked over to Zaid, dagger out.

They were going to kill him first.

"No," Kinza rasped out. Zaid had to get out. This had nothing to do with him. He didn't deserve this. "Stop!" she shrieked, but Jafar only nodded to the two other men. They grabbed Zaid by the arms and hauled him upright. Panic was starting to make her tremble. Zaid tried to thrash more, but he was too weak and could barely move.

Please stop. Please stop. Please stop. Her mind was flying, trying to find a way out; the forest, the river, the sky. There was nothing, though. In her panic, she launched to her feet in Zaid's direction, but Yusuf wrenched her back, grabbing onto her arms. She scrabbled her feet into the dirt, trying to get a purchase. She only succeeded in digging into the ground.

Ghufran held Zaid's head back, exposing his already blood-soaked neck as Jafar stepped forward.

"Stop, please stop!" she cried out loud this time. *"Please!"* she shrieked.

Kinza, Zaid's voice said in her head. The sorrow in it only made her cry louder. *Kinza, I'm sorry.*

The finality of it sent her over the edge. The heat built to a crescendo in her abdomen, and a white light turned everything to day.

CHAPTER 19
BURNING LIGHTS

The trickling light from the sun over the treetops was nothing compared to the light that erupted around her. Kinza couldn't hear anything but felt herself scream, in rage and in pain. A sonic boom ripped through the clearing in one heartbeat leaving behind a sound so loud she thought the atoms in her body would break apart. She didn't realize when she stopped screaming.

The light faded before the sound did; it held like a single note being played by a god, rippling through the air. It sent birds all throughout the forest bursting into the sky in a cloud of feathers. But eventually, that faded too, and Kinza opened her eyes.

The first thing she saw was the fire. The pits around her had gone out, but the treetops around the clearing were burning, sending black smoke into the air. The white light had faded but was replaced by the burning forest. Fiery branches fell to the ground, setting the forest floor alight as well. It would be moments before the smoke got to her lungs; she needed to move.

She struggled to stand. Her joints had locked up, and her ribs ached from Yusuf's boot. She looked behind her, and his body lay prone on the ground, blood trickling out of his ears and nose. Kinza looked toward the others and saw Rafiq on the ground already, arms clutching his ears before going limp a moment later. Jafar was screaming through gritted teeth, but he, too, fell. Blood streamed out of every orifice in his face until eventually, he stopped moving, eyes wide open.

Just beyond them was Zaid, face down in the dirt. "Zaid!" she tried to yell, but almost no sound came out. Her voice was raw. The fire was creeping toward the clearing, and smoke started to get into her eyes. *Zaid!* she said it in her mind this time. Sure enough, he started to move. His shoulders rolled like a lion as he tried to push himself up. Kinza started to crawl toward him, coughing at the smoke.

He looked up, looking for her. He caught sight of her quickly and started to move, but he was still badly wounded and hardly moved an inch.

She made it only a few feet when a dark form stumbled out of the trees to the right of him. Zaid saw her line of sight and screamed into her mind, *Kinza, run!*

Ghufran lurched out of the trees holding an arm up beneath his nose. The cloth around his head had been ripped away, and she could see the sharp, angular lines of his face. Blood streamed out of his eyes and ears, but not as much as the others. A look of rage came over him at the sight of her and their surroundings. He grabbed an obsidian dagger that had fallen to the ground and started toward her.

Kinza was too frightened to move. She sat there as Ghufran came at her, dagger raised, only to freeze in that position a few feet from her. His look of rage turned to one of shock as he looked down. An obsidian sword protruded from his chest. The sword was wrenched out, and Ghufran's body fell to the ground.

Aisha stood behind him with the bloody sword. She was dripping wet as if she had just come from the river. Kinza tried to scramble back as Aisha took a step toward her.

"Get back!" Kinza rasped, some sound coming out now. She coughed again, and her eyes watered from the smoke. She had to get Zaid and leave.

Aisha stopped and dropped the sword to the ground. Putting her hands up, she said, "I'm not going to hurt you," as if placating a wounded animal. Kinza gave no indication she believed her and stayed where she was. She could see Zaid coughing on the other side of the clearing. The sun was near to the tops of the trees now. It sent beams of light through the thickening smoke.

Aisha reached up and pulled the cloth around her face down. She had light brown skin, similar to Kinza's own, but a narrow jawline and wide eyes. It made her look startled. "Kinza, I'm not going to kill you. What Jafar told you about the prophecy was not right. It was only part of it. There are people in Rhapta who have been waiting for you for a long time." She crouched down to the ground bringing herself closer to Kinza. She had a look of reverence on her face as she reached out toward her.

"Get away from me!" Kinza screamed. She couldn't believe a word she said. She just wanted to get Zaid and leave. It didn't matter what Jafar said anymore.

Kinza's reaction had shocked the woman out of her position, standing up again. She gave one wary nod and turned and dove into the river. She didn't see her rise as the water moved downstream.

As soon as she was sure the woman was gone, Kinza scrambled to her feet, staying low. Her ribs barked in protest, but she ignored them and stumbled past Ghufran and Jafar's bodies to Zaid. She was thankful he was still alive, if only barely. She grabbed him under the chest and heaved upward. He groaned but sat up and looked at her. The one eye was starting to heal but slowly. He had also stopped bleeding, but she was sure he was still weary from blood loss and the healing lacerations. She wouldn't be surprised if he had several broken bones. The sight of him made her want to cry again.

We have to go, she said to him, not trusting her voice.

He nodded weakly. That was enough for her, and she put one of his arms around her shoulders and wrapped one of hers around his waist. The next part was difficult. Zaid groaned again as she hauled him to his feet with strength she didn't know was there. They both coughed again, the smoke was thick, and the clearing was truly burning now.

They stumbled into the forest as quickly as they could, but Zaid was more injured than Kinza had thought. He could hardly lift his feet, and his head drooped forward. She stopped a few feet away, looking around. She hadn't seen where the assassins had taken her and didn't know the way back to the car. Zaid was no help as he was barely holding on. She decided to follow the direction of the river and walked as fast as she could. The smoke was reaching toward her through the trees. She just wanted to get away from the fire, and then they could rest.

They went on like that for twenty minutes, but Zaid's steps had become even more sluggish, and Kinza's ribs were on fire. She leaned to the side when she could no longer hold him up. She let him fall to the ground gently. She sat there coughing. Zaid had passed out, but they were outside of the line of smoke for the moment. It wouldn't last long, though.

What was she supposed to do? They weren't going to make it at the rate they were going. Fear started to grip her again as she saw flames several feet out between the trees. She sat next to Zaid with one hand on his chest and looked down at him. She needed to get him out of here.

An idea sparked in her mind.

Looking back at the flames, she let fear take over her heart, and it started pounding a little faster, but she didn't let herself fall into the deep panic she had in the clearing. Closing her eyes, she thought of the car they had left tucked off the side of the road. It couldn't have been that far.

Her heart beat once, twice, and on the third beat, she felt the roots underneath her shift. She opened her eyes and almost cried at the sight of the car before them and the road beyond.

She had teleported! On purpose! And *with* another person. She would tell Zaid about it later, but for now, she gulped a large breath of clean air and struggled with him back to their feet. His eyes blinked open and closed, but he did as best he could as she shoved him into the back of the car, laying him across the seats.

When she closed the door, she saw Aisha standing by the front of the car. Kinza tensed and took a step back.

"Please, just hear me out," the woman said, palms out. Kinza just noticed she had the same accent as the others, the same as Zaid. She didn't move but watched the woman for any sudden movements. Not that it would help her much, she was dead on her feet. "You are both injured and have nowhere to go. Do not lie to me," she said as Kinza started to speak. "Let me help you. I know of a safe place close by, a thirty-minute drive toward Moshi. You can rest on the way."

Kinza looked her over. The woman had protested back in the clearing when Jafar was torturing them, but she hadn't actually done anything to stop it. Kinza didn't believe her little story about the prophecy either. On the other hand, she was right. They had nowhere to go, and they desperately needed someplace safe to rest.

"I know you don't trust me, but you really don't have another option."

Kinza hesitated before relenting. "Fine, but I'm driving."

The woman pursed her lips, clearly unhappy with that idea, but gave a single nod. They climbed into the car and pulled onto the road.

Later Kinza wouldn't remember the drive in detail, she was too delirious, but she wanted to keep some measure of control while Aisha was in the car with them. She stayed quiet in the passenger's seat, only speaking to give directions. After half an hour, they pulled into a driveway in a quiet neighborhood. A small house sat behind a line of trees, and it looked dark inside.

Good. Kinza didn't want to be around other people right now.

It took both of them working together to haul Zaid into the house. It consisted of one main living area, a small kitchen, a bathroom, and a single bedroom. It was sparsely furnished as if no one lived there regularly. They dropped Zaid onto one side of the bed, and he didn't move, breathing deeply.

"I will leave you for now, but I will come back with bandages and clothes," Aisha said. Kinza nodded, not caring what she did. The door closed quietly on her way out.

Once the woman left, Kinza looked over Zaid's injuries. None of them were profusely bleeding, but they still looked pretty bad, and she didn't know what kind of internal injuries he had. Unfortunately, there was nothing else she could do at the moment.

At least she had gotten them to temporary safety. She would just have to hope Anunnaki healing worked fast. As she curled up on the other side of the bed, she was asleep before her head hit the pillow.

WHEN KINZA OPENED her eyes again, the room was lit only by a small lamp in the corner. The sky through the window above her was dark. How long had she slept? She turned over and saw Zaid was awake.

He was sitting on the other edge of the bed fiddling with one of his knives. Where had he had that? Was it on him this whole time? Some things about him remained a mystery to her.

He looked up and grunted when he saw she was awake as well. "How are you feeling?" he asked, looking back down at his knife. Kinza almost thought she had dreamed how badly he had been hurt with what he looked like now. He was wearing new clothes, a light gray t-shirt, and black cargo pants. Both eyes were open, and no cuts lined his face and arms. She breathed a sigh of relief.

Kinza sat up gingerly, expecting herself to be in pain, but it was the same with her. Her ribs no longer hurt, and her throat wasn't raw anymore. She felt better, if still a bit tired. "I think I'm okay. What about you?"

A wry smile appeared, and his eyes crinkled in amusement. "It seems I was the damsel in distress, and I was rescued by a very effective knight." He looked up at her, gentle laughter in his eyes. She gave him a wry smile right back.

The memory of the car ride to the house came back to her, and she glanced toward the doorway.

"She's not here, but—" he started to say, but Kinza cut him off.

"I'm sorry," she said, looking down at her hands in her lap. She needed to say this before the moment passed. "I'm sorry for what I said to you. It was horrible and wrong, and I didn't even mean it. I was just... trying to be mean, I guess." When he didn't say anything, she peeked up at him, ready for wrath, but only incredulity met her.

"After what happened last night, *that's* what you want to talk about?" he asked.

She was sure the other things could wait. "Yes," she said, nodding. "I didn't want you to think that I meant them."

"I forgive you, but now it's my turn. What Jafar said wasn't entirely true, about the prophecy."

She looked back down at her lap. "I don't really care."

"You should, because while he didn't tell the whole truth, it's a very real possibility that he was right."

Kinza flinched.

"Just listen," Zaid said and sighed. "Rhapta has many prophecies, and it is true this is probably the biggest one, but it was vaguer than that. It says someone, an outsider, will come to the city and either bring destruction *or* return it to its former glory and save our people from dying out. It's not definitive on which, and many people believe it is up to that person to decide what they will do.

"And while it's true that some underground groups want that person dead, there are just as many, if not more people who are eagerly awaiting that person. I hadn't heard about Hakim's recent vision, it could have even been after I left the last time, but if he mentioned a larger tattoo like yours, then it's very possible. And you do seem to have unusual abilities."

"Would that explain why I'm just getting them now then?" She didn't truly want to think about the prophecy. That was a little too much to handle right at that moment.

"Yes, actually it could. The prophecy doesn't really explain who the person is or why they exist outside of Rhapta, so it could be any number of things."

"So he wasn't lying then," she asked quietly, "when he said all that stuff about my parents; my mother?"

"I don't think so," he said softly. "I am truly sorry, Kinza."

She nodded and accepted that she at least knew the truth. It didn't stop her lip from quivering as her eyes filled with tears. She looked down at her hands, hoping the tears wouldn't fall.

Zaid ducked his head to look at her through her curtain of hair that had fallen. *It'll be okay, Kinza,* he said inside her mind. She realized how close it felt to have someone in there with her, and for a second, she felt less alone. The dam holding back her tears gave way, and she wept into her lap. Zaid's arms came around her then, pulling her into his chest. She wept into his shirt for what had been done to her parents. For Grams who had to live through the death of her daughter. For the hell she had inadvertently put Zaid through this last week. And for herself and the unfairness of the world. She knew you weren't supposed to feel sorry for yourself, but she did. She felt sorry for the things in her life she had missed out on, for lack of parents or money, and for the ugliness that was this prophecy.

The whole time she cried, Zaid muttered softly in the same language from the night before. Eventually, exhaustion crept back over her, and she fell back into the pit of sleep.

ZAID TUCKED the blanket around Kinza. She was still in her bloody clothes from the night before, but there was nothing to do about it now.

He walked back out to the living room, reflecting on his own stupidity. He should have listened to Haris when he had mentioned the prophecy. Zaid had never been one to follow them in the way his mother did. They had never affected his life before; certainly not like this. But now, the sleeping girl in the other room could very likely be the person from the most notable prophecy in all of Rhapta.

What would happen when he brought her back to Rhapta? Would there be people waiting to kill her? No, he wouldn't let that happen. It might even be best to go in through the slums first.

Zaid sighed, feeling more tired than he had in a long time. It was night again, they had slept all day, and he had only woken an hour ago. At first, he had panicked, not knowing where he was, but then he had heard Kinza's soft breathing next to him, and his panic subsided.

Looking through the kitchen, there wasn't much to eat. There had been clothes, bandages, and water in the living room when he had woken. He vaguely remembered the woman, Aisha, carrying him with Kinza into the house. She must have dropped the stuff off. Kinza would wake again soon and would be wanting food again. After checking on her one more time, he stepped out of the house into the night.

He moved through the streets to the center of town, avoiding streetlights and headlights. It didn't really matter, no one would have seen him, but he wanted to be careful. His duffel bag was somewhere in the forest, and that meant he had to steal food instead of paying for it. He moved quickly, taking a premade order sitting on a vendor's window before anyone saw him. He made a mental note to pay the shop owner back in the future. He was gone no more than five minutes and stepped back in the house.

Aisha was sitting in the living room.

What are you doing here? he snapped. Even if she had helped bring them back, he couldn't trust her.

I had come back to see if either of you were awake. There are things you should know. She sat on the couch as if she owned the place. On second thought, she probably did.

"How considerate of you. I should have been told a lot of things this week." He said it louder than he should have. A moment later, Kinza's heartbeat quickened in the other room into wakefulness. He berated himself for being so loud.

"I am not in charge of *venari*. Savar and Ishar are, but from what I understand, Tahir is a mentor of yours even though he does not represent the *venari*?" she asked. Zaid could hear Kinza changing in the other room.

"Yes, he helped me out a few times when I was younger, and we have remained close. I'm bringing Kinza to see him when we get back." Just then, Kinza stepped out from the bedroom. Aisha had brought her a t-shirt and a patterned wrap skirt that could be found at just about any market. Her eyes went right to Aisha and narrowed.

"I was just telling Zaid that there are things you ought to know before you go to Rhapta," Aisha said to her. She turned to Zaid. "One of which is not to trust Tahir."

That statement did nothing to help his suspicion of her. He crossed his arms. "What? No. He is going to help Kinza, and he'll keep the more violent groups away from her."

"He was the one who did this," she replied.

"Did what? Tahir has only been good to my family and me. It sounds like you are trying to cut us off."

"Boy, you are not listening to me. Do not trust Tahir. *He is the one who sent us,*" she said, leaning forward.

Zaid thought he heard wrong for a second. "Tahir? The Elder Tahir? You must have mistaken—"

"I'm not playing these games!" Aisha shouted. "I am here to warn you. He was the one who got the prophecy from Hakim. He was the one who sent us to kill her." She pointed at Kinza. "And told us to either do it before you got there or kill you if we didn't." She stood. "I am leaving to deal with the bodies by the river." She looked toward Kinza, and her eyes gentled. "I meant what I said about the people in the city who are waiting for you. We have needed you for a long time."

Kinza only stared back in confusion. Aisha didn't seem to notice. She nodded once toward Zaid and left out the front door, vanishing into the night.

Kinza moved and sat on the spot Aisha had just left. She still looked tired. "Is Tahir the person you told me about before? The one you were bringing me to?" she asked. He sat down on a chair across the room.

"Yes." Could Aisha's claim have any merit? No. He had known Tahir for years and had helped him time and again.

"Would he really do that?"

Zaid looked over at her. The light from the bedroom was the only illumination and cast her face into soft shadows. "No, he wouldn't." He took a deep breath. "But just to be safe, we'll enter through the outskirts of the city, the slums. My friend Khalil lives there; he's a healer. We can go to him first, and he can keep our presence unknown until we figure out what the hell is happening." He rubbed his hands over his face.

When he opened his eyes, Kinza was staring at him. He realized she had gone from looking at him with pure terror, to savage hatred, to open trust in just a few days. It seemed like a feat in itself. Maybe she could actually do something to help his people.

She yawned and stood back up. "Okay then, I'm still exhausted, so I'm going back to sleep. I assume we are headed back to the mountain in the morning?"

He nodded, and she padded back into the room. After she had fallen back asleep, Zaid spent the next few hours awake, going over every memory he had of Tahir.

CHAPTER 20

DESTINY'S DESTRUCTION

Kinza's foot bounced on the dash in time with the radio. When the morning had come, it had brought with it a sense of renewal for her. While none of the bad stuff from the night before had gone away, she felt less like she was drowning this morning.

Zaid drove them back down the highway in their stolen car. Before they left town, they had checked and found out someone had seen the fire, and it had been put out before it could spread too far. She was thankful she didn't burn down an entire mountain.

Zaid looked over at her, the sunlight dappling through the window onto his face and chest. He looked at her quizzically, though, and turned the radio down. "I have to ask you something about last night."

She raised her eyebrows at him in question, hoping he would talk faster. She liked this song and wanted to turn it back up.

"How did we get from the river back to the car? I don't

remember any of that, so I must've blacked out. Did you carry me?"

Kinza laughed. "Even better," she said, grinning at him. When he didn't understand, she said, "I teleported us!"

It was Zaid's turn to raise his eyebrows. "All by yourself? On purpose?" He turned back to the road, looking slightly impressed. He turned to her again, "Were we falling for any reason?"

She snorted and smacked him on the arm. "No, we were just at the risk of burning to death or running out of oxygen. Apparently, that works just as well."

They drove along the highway and took the side road north again. They had to stop a little sooner as official vehicles lined the road where they had stopped the night before. Zaid pulled over, putting his hazards on, and parked the car under a tree. He spent a few minutes covering it up with leaves.

"So we have to walk all the way back like yesterday?" she asked. While she was happy about the bright morning, the sun had brought the heat back with it, and she was already sweating. Aisha had also only brought her a pair of sandals as her sneakers were soaked with Zaid's blood. It was nice to walk in clean shoes, but they weren't great for traipsing through the forest.

"Actually, it's light enough that I can just run. C'mon, hop on my back." He turned and crouched a little for her to get on.

"Really?" Kinza asked with a laugh. She didn't wait and launched herself onto his back, causing him to grunt a little. He just sighed and started walking.

She didn't know what to expect when Zaid said he was going to run, but she gasped once they got inside the tree line. Suddenly everything moved by in a blur of green and brown. For fear of falling off, she gripped him around his shoulders and held on tight and prayed that she didn't vomit all over him.

He ran for close to twenty minutes, and she had to marvel at the fact she didn't know anyone who could run at top speed while carrying another person; human or Anunnaki. They finally stopped in what looked like just another cluster of trees within the forest.

"We'll walk from here. It's just up ahead." Kinza followed behind him as they started pushing through the vines and foliage. She tripped less this time, but still more than him, if he tripped at all. As they got closer, she started to feel a faint hum coming from up ahead. The only other times she had heard it was in her nightmares, and now she found her feet would move no further.

Zaid got a few steps before turning around. "What's wrong?" he asked, brow wrinkling.

"I'm not sure," she said honestly. Something just felt *wrong*. Not that she was necessarily in danger, but just off.

Zaid walked back over to her and grabbed her hand. It was warm and old calluses scraped against her skin. *We're almost there, and then we can relax,* he said in her mind. She nodded, but the uneasiness didn't subside.

He tugged her forward, and she followed, still holding his hand. It was a small reassurance as she caught sight of the barrier in front of them. Just as in her dreams, it shimmered in the air, not unlike the portals. He looked back just before he went through, and she held her breath.

Unlike the portal, she didn't vomit. In fact, the only thing she felt was a slight tugging sensation, and then she was through, still within the trees.

Not so bad, right? Zaid asked.

Yeah, I've had worse. She gave him a slight grin trying to lighten the mood, but the same feeling prodded at her even more now that they had passed through.

They walked through the trees, Zaid just slightly ahead when suddenly he stopped dead in his tracks. Kinza caught up to him, a look of blatant fear written across his face. He dropped her hand.

She looked to what had drawn his gaze. Just ahead past the tree line, she could see a large swathe of ramshackle huts and beyond them rose the city of Rhapta. Massive limestone buildings that stretched further than she could see.

But each of them had walls that had crumbled or were stained with black soot. Many of the huts had been leveled, and food and clothes scattered on the ground. Smoke still rose all around the city, but it looked to be the remnants of a fire that had ended days ago. Not a single soul could be seen. They heard not a single sound.

Kinza and Zaid looked on in horror. Rhapta had been destroyed.

EPILOGUE

Tahir moved through the tunnel, holding a lit torch out in front of him to light his way. It wasn't so deep underground as to hide from the screams that came down from up above. Even to him, Anunnaki using their voices was an eerie sound, especially as they were dying.

He moved quicker, surrounded by warriors both in front and behind him, the ones loyal to him anyway. They paused at an intersection. In the front of the line, a warrior kicked at a short man they had shackled between them. He yelped and then said reluctantly, *Left*. Tahir was glad he hadn't killed Hunar as well. He had proved his usefulness over the last seven years, whether he enjoyed his participation or not. The procession started down the left hall.

The man had dared speak out against him in public. It took less effort than breathing to have his reputation verily ruined. He had been forced into poverty and eventually to the outskirts of the city. Tahir had smiled at the thought of him there, *speaking* aloud like the rest of the animals. That was until Tahir had needed him again, so back into the fold he came.

The screams were getting fainter to Tahir's relief. It meant they were getting closer to the end. He almost regretted what he had done. The city was glorious, but there were things he had to do, things the other Elders refused to do, all to keep the Anunnaki line alive. Sometimes you needed to cull the herd to save it.

Eventually, they came to the end, and a large iron door took up the entire hallway. Tahir pushed men out of the way as he swept forward. Ice crept over the hinges to the lock, freezing it. It cracked and fell to the floor. He stepped back and allowed the others to open it for him.

As he went through, he passed by Hunar, who glared up at him. The poor man looked like a petulant child in his too-big robes and pinched face. *Come now, Hunar. Be thankful you are one of those who gets to live. There is much work to do.* The last part was more to himself than anything.

He stalked out of the tunnel into the night, white robes fluttering around him. Warriors swarmed out of the tunnel into the trees, checking for anyone waiting. There would be no one, of course. The ones he needed had already left, and those he didn't remained in the city.

Tahir looked back, and in the distance, he could see smoke rising about the firelight in the city. The screams were too far to hear individually. It was more of a hum now. Not for the first time, he wondered if he should feel some kind of remorse as he looked upon his home. It had stood for longer than any human civilization.

He turned with disinterest and walked deeper into the forest, the others following behind him.

GLOSSARY OF TERMS

abilities *(ah bill it ees) n.* Powers that each Anunnaki has. The abilities vary per person and are supernatural in nature.

Anunnaki *(ahn new nock ee) n.* A species thought to have originated from Rhapta to guide humanity. They live longer than humans, can speak to each other telepathically, and have abilities. They reside only in Rhapta. If an Anunnaki leaves the city limits, their abilities fade, and they slowly become human and forget Rhapta. Some live outside the city limits but still within the psychic barrier. Their abilities are weakened, and they have developed a need for verbal speech.

Elder *(ell der) n.* One of the fifty leaders of Rhapta. One out of every fifty is a Grand Elder who leads in ceremony and prophecy.

guakal *(gwa kall) n.* A fist-sized, rigid-shelled, lime-green fruit with miniature red spikes on its exterior; native to Rhapta.

laqueus *(la kwees) n.* A rope, silvery-gray in color, made by Anunnaki used to bind or dampen abilities. Mildly annoying to Anunnaki, physically painful to humans.

magalkan'a *(muh gal kahn uh) n.* Commonly known as Aurastone, believed to be the origin of Anunnaki abilities. Shades range from white to azure.

mark *(mar k) n.* The tribal tattoo that every Anunnaki is born with. Only *venari* and ubir have different tattoos. *Venari's* are larger and need to be reapplied monthly; it allows them to enter the human world while retaining their abilities for a short time. Ubir tattoos are similar but red and swollen, as if infected.

reykalkan'o *(ray kal kon oh) n.* Commonly known as Deathstone. It is cracked Aurastone. Created either by blood magic, or taking it from Rhapta. Its presence is extremely painful to Anunnaki, creating a high-pitched ringing. If the Anunnaki cannot hear it, it's unlikely to be harmful.

Rhapta *(rap tuh) n.* An ancient city located near Mt. Kilimanjaro. It is hidden behind a psychic barrier and unknown to humanity. Currently at half capacity due to its dwindling population.

ubir *(oo beer) n.* Anunnaki that have defected from Rhapta and turned to blood magic to exist outside of the city while retaining their abilities. They quickly become rabid and need to sacrifice humans to retain their abilities. Their Aura is chaotic and painful.

Ummanu *(oo mon oo) n.* Humans who are aware of Anunnaki's existence and have allied with them. Most watch over the portals around the world.

venari *(venn are ee) n.* Anunnaki bounty hunters tasked with locating and returning ubir from human society. They are shunned within Rhapta due to their "dirty" work and closeness with human society.

Author's Note

Author's Note

Dear Beloved Reader,

I'm so thankful and humbled that you took the time to read my very first published book, Cryptic Magic! The readers of this first book will always hold a special place in my heart. I'm so excited about this series, and I hope you enjoyed reading about Kinza and Zaid. If you did, I would be so grateful if you would consider leaving a review. Reviews help other readers find my work, and each review means the world to me.

I know the cliffhanger at the end of this book may have left you a little shaken, but I'm excited to announce that Book 2, Erratic Magic, is listed on Amazon, so be sure to get your copy!

I've published a new novella that is only available to those who sign up for my mailing list! Portal Magic: A Rhaptaverse Novella is a glimpse into my upcoming Rhaptaverse series which will show the new batch of venari as they go out into the human world to save humanity from the ubir. You absolutely don't want to miss it! Click here (https://swiy.co/Portal Magic) to download your copy today.

Please be sure to visit my website LilySkyy.com. There's awesome merch available for each of my series. While you're there, make sure to sign up for my mailing list to be the first to know about new releases and special happenings such as previews and give-a-ways!

I love getting feedback from my readers, and if you'd like to stay in touch (or just vent about the ending of Cryptic Magic), join me over at the Lily Skyy Reader's Group. I'd also love to connect with you on Instagram, TikTok, and Twitter! Feel free to reach out to me directly via email at social@lilyskyy.com. You can find all my social media profiles by visiting: https://smartpa.ge/lilyskyy.

Again, I thank you for reading, and I can't wait to join you on the next adventure!

Sincerely,

Lily Skyy

9 781960 207425